THE DARK KNIGHT™

THE DARK KNIGHT™

Novelization by Dennis O'Neil

Screenplay by
Jonathan Nolan and Christopher Nolan

Story by
Christopher Nolan & David S. Goyer

Batman created by Bob Kane

BERKLEY BOULEVARD BOOKS, NEW YORK

THE BERKLEY PUBLISHING GROUP
Published by the Penguin Group
Penguin Group (USA) Inc.
375 Hudson Street, New York, New York 10014, USA

Penguin Group (Canada), 90 Eglinton Avenue East, Suite 700, Toronto, Ontario M4P 2Y3, Canada
(a division of Pearson Penguin Canada Inc.)
Penguin Books Ltd., 80 Strand, London WC2R 0RL, England
Penguin Group Ireland, 25 St. Stephen's Green, Dublin 2, Ireland (a division of Penguin Books Ltd.)
Penguin Group (Australia), 250 Camberwell Road, Camberwell, Victoria 3124, Australia
(a division of Pearson Australia Group Pty. Ltd.)
Penguin Books India Pvt. Ltd., 11 Community Centre, Panchsheel Park, New Delhi—110 017, India
Penguin Group (NZ), 67 Apollo Drive, Rosedale, North Shore 0632, New Zealand
(a division of Pearson New Zealand Ltd.)
Penguin Books (South Africa) (Pty.) Ltd., 24 Sturdee Avenue, Rosebank, Johannesburg 2196,
South Africa

Penguin Books Ltd., Registered Offices: 80 Strand, London WC2R 0RL, England

This is a work of fiction. Names, characters, places, and incidents either are the product of the author's imagination or are used fictitiously, and any resemblance to actual persons, living or dead, business establishments, events, or locales is entirely coincidental. The publisher does not have any control over and does not assume any responsibility for author or third-party websites or their content.

THE DARK KNIGHT

A Berkley Boulevard Book / published by arrangement with DC Comics

PRINTING HISTORY
Berkley Boulevard mass-market movie tie-in edition / July 2008

ISBN: 978-0-425-22286-7

BERKLEY BOULEVARD®
Berkley Boulevard Books are published by The Berkley Publishing Group,
a division of Penguin Group (USA) Inc.,
375 Hudson Street, New York, New York 10014.
BERKLEY BOULEVARD is a registered trademark of Penguin Group (USA) Inc.
The BERKLEY BOULEVARD logo is a trademark belonging to Penguin Group (USA) Inc.

PRINTED IN THE UNITED STATES OF AMERICA

10 9 8 7 6 5 4 3 2 1

To the memories of
Walter Gibson and Bill Finger
They got there first.

ACKNOWLEDGMENTS

He continues to evolve, this dark-cloaked avenger, this tragic lurker in shadows, as he has been evolving for decades now, and that constant, gradual change may be why the old gent is as healthy as he's ever been. The book you hold, and the movie it's adapted from, are the latest iterations of the ongoing Batman saga, and some acknowledgments are in order:

The story is by Christopher Nolan and David S. Goyer, and the screenplay is by Jonathan Nolan and Christopher Nolan. Their work speaks for itself. I merely followed their lead.

Again, I nod gratefully to Chris Cerasi, gentleman and editor.

Marifran, who was once named McFarland and has been an O'Neil for twenty years now, was, as always, the cheerleader who alleviates what can be a lonely business.

Dennis O'Neil
Nyack, New York
February 2008

ONE

It was both a memory and a nightmare . . .

Batman reached the lead car, swayed for a moment as he considered his options, and decided that he could not afford to waste time strategizing. He had to operate in the moment, letting instinct guide him.

He might have only seconds left.

He sat on the edge of the car and swung his legs backward. His boots struck a shatterproof window and knocked it from its frame. As it dropped to one of the seats, Batman was already sliding and twisting through the empty frame and landing inside the car. He landed in a crouch on the floor facing the front of the train. A shadow on the floor alerted him that he was being attacked from behind and, without taking time to turn, he drove his elbow backward. It connected with the face of one of Rā's al Ghūl's men, who stumbled toward the car's rear door.

The microwave transmitter blocked the aisle, humming and vibrating slightly. Behind it stood Rā's al Ghūl.

"You're still not dead," Ra's said.

"Obviously not. We can end this now, Rā's. There's no need for further bloodshed."

"Oh, you are wrong, Bruce. There's an enormous need."

"I'll stop you."

"No, you won't. Because to stop me you would have to kill me, and you will not do that."

"You're sure?"

"Yes. You could not stand to see another father die." Rā's edged around the machine and slid his sword from the cane. "But I have seen many of my children die. Another one won't make much difference to me."

Rā's advanced, the sword in one hand, the cane in the other. He feinted with the sword and swung the cane at Batman's head. Batman trapped it in one of his scallops, twisted his arm, and the cane went spinning over his shoulder.

Rā's thrust the sword point at Batman's chest. Batman pivoted, and the steel slipped past his chest, grazing his costume. Rā's kicked. Batman sidestepped and Rā's kicked again, striking Batman's hip. As Batman stumbled, trying to regain his footing, Rā's arced the blade downward toward Batman's head, but he crossed his wrists and trapped the steel in the scallops of both gauntlets.

"Familiar," Rā's said. "Don't you have anything new?"

"How about this?" *Batman yanked his arms in opposite directions and the blade snapped in two. Then Batman drove the palm of his right hand into Rā's al Ghūl's chest, and, as Rā's stumbled backward, Batman jumped onto a seat and past Rā's to the train controls.*

He looked out the front window and saw Wayne Tower looming ahead. He grabbed the brake lever, but before he could pull it back, Rā's shoved his cane into the mechanism, jamming it. Before Batman could free it, Rā's swung his clenched fists at the back of Batman's head, bouncing it off the windshield. Rā's struck again, and Batman fell and rolled onto his back. Rā's was straddling him, his hands clenched around Batman's neck, his thumbs pressing into Batman's throat.

"Don't be afraid, Bruce . . . you hate this city as much as I do, but you're just an ordinary man in a cape. That's why you can't fight injustice in this city . . . and that's why you can't stop this train."

"Who said anything about stopping it?"

The train car shook and Rā's al Ghūl's grasp relaxed for an instant. He looked through the windshield at the track, twisted and smoking.

"You'll never learn to mind your surroundings," Batman said, "as much as your opponent." He slammed his

right gauntlet into Rā's al Ghūl's face. Rā's toppled side-ways, and Batman scrambled to his feet. He grabbed his opponent's hair with his left hand and pulled a scalloped Batarang from under his cloak with his right. He raised the weapon over his head; a single downward swing would bury it in Rā's al Ghūl's skull.

Rā's smiled. "Have you finally learned to do what is necessary?"

Batman flung the weapon at the windshield. The glass cracked, then broke. "I won't kill you . . ."

Batman pulled a small grenade from his belt and threw it at the back door of the car. There was an explo-sion, and the door was gone.

"But I don't have to save you."

Batman moved to the other side of the microwave transmitter and thrust his hands into his cape. It stiff-ened and became a wing.

Batman caught a thermal, which lifted him a couple hundred feet into the air. He looked down. There was a fire gouting up the wall of the Tower, and in it, he could see the silhouette of the monorail car. To the south, he saw the flashing red lights of fire engines and heard the distant wail of sirens, mingled with the sighing of the wind . . .

Bruce Wayne opened his eyes and, for a moment, let the nightmare that was a memory fade, then sat up in his bed, feeling the pleasant silkiness of the sheets against his bare skin. He swung his legs onto the floor, stood, walked to the window. In the glow of the eastern sky, he could see, on the street below, the burned remains of a large chunk of the monorail leading to Wayne Tower—the only remaining visible reminder of his battle with Rā's al Ghūl.

For him, it had been the end of a long journey.

He could not say what the real beginning of that journey was. The time, in early childhood, when he'd been playing in the yard with Rachel Dawes and fell into a well, breaking the wall and loosing the thousands of bats that lived in the cave beyond?

The ordeal hadn't lasted long. Within a minute, two at most, Thomas Wayne had climbed down a rope, enfolded his son in strong arms, and taken him back to sunlight. But that short time alone, in the cold and dark, with the monstrosities flapping around him, was grim, would have left a scar on any child's memory.

But the worst was still ahead. The worst was the night when Bruce and his father and mother were walking on a side street after watching an opera performance and a mugger had murdered Bruce's parents.

Two pulls of a trigger—*bang bang*—and Mother's pearls were spilling into the gutter, stained with her blood, Father lying sprawled next to her. Bruce listened to the sound of the mugger's running feet on the pavement and knew, to an absolute certainty, that his life had changed forever.

Was *that* the real beginning? Yes. Surely, something

else was born the instant his parents fell, and Bruce Wayne—whoever he was, whatever he might have become—was extinguished.

But there were other moments, ones that accelerated the process, the transformation that had begun with the death of the Waynes.

His impulsive decision to leave Gotham City: Bruised and bleeding from an encounter with Carmine Falcone, he ran across the rotting board of a dock, cold fog in his face and the smell of decaying fish in his nostrils, and leapt, grabbed a chain trailing from the stern of a rusty freighter and climbed aboard, beginning an odyssey that took him deep into the underbelly of civilization. He met and mingled with the angry and insane beings who preyed on their fellows, the thieves and sadists and murderers, trying to understand them, eventually becoming one of them . . .

The meeting with Rā's al Ghūl: It was in a prison cell. Bruce had been consigned to solitary confinement after he had severely injured several other prisoners in a mess-hall brawl. The tall, solemn man offered Bruce not only release, but redemption. Bruce accepted, and soon became an acolyte of the most dangerous man on Earth . . .

The years at the monastery: Rā's was his master, Rā's was his savior, and in the monastery, unknown to the world, high in the Himalayas, Bruce learned the mental discipline and physical skills that made him nearly invincible in combat. The training was harsh and merciless; mistakes were not tolerated and usually resulted in death. But those who survived were something just shy of supermen, and of them all, Bruce was the best. He imagined that he would live as Rā's al Ghūl's servant for quite some times until he learned that Ra's planned to save humanity by slaughtering tens of millions, beginning with the citizens of Gotham City . . .

He had help from others—from Rachel Dawes, childhood friend and sweetheart, whose quiet idealism inspired him, and Lucius Fox, who supplied him with the tools and technology he needed, and Alfred, his closest friend and constant advisor, and even his ancestors, the Wayne dynasty, who were kind enough to amass the vast fortune that financed his activities.

That money enabled young Bruce to give himself a first-rate education. Until he was twelve, he attended the best private schools in the area. Then, when a principal told Alfred that there was "nothing more we can give the lad," he studied with a series of tutors. In science, he was always excellent. In languages, also excellent. In history, so-so. In social sciences, fair, and in liberal arts, mediocre, except in drama; he loved to read plays, and when he learned that Alfred had once been a child actor in Great Britain, he asked a lot of questions, especially how performers achieved their effects.

By Bruce's fourteenth year, Alfred got used to looking out one of the big windows of the mansion and seeing young Bruce running around the grounds, climbing and swinging from trees, sometimes just throwing rocks, hard and far. Bruce heard of a local soccer league for young folks that had just formed in the neighborhood, and, although he was not enrolled in any of the local schools, he managed to join one of the teams. He quit after his second practice. "Guess I'm just not the locker-room type," he told Alfred, and never mentioned the subject again.

But he didn't abandon sports, just teams. When he was sixteen he asked Alfred if they could go skiing. Alfred had never been near a ski slope, but he made some calls and learned of an excellent, though pricey, resort in Vermont and phoned for reservations there and went shopping for equipment.

They decided to drive, which was a mistake. A bad blizzard struck, and driving became both slow and hazardous. They didn't manage to check in until after ten. The pretty young woman at the desk said that the ski lifts were closed for the night and wouldn't open again until six, but that the lounge was open, where there was a roaring fire going, and plenty of good company. Alfred thought that sounded pretty good, but Bruce begged off—too tired, he said. Alfred bade him good night and went into the lounge where, for an extremely pleasant hour, he drank hot cider and chatted with a retired schoolteacher whose hobby was growing begonias.

Alfred decided to look in on Bruce before retiring. He found Bruce's room empty, the bed unslept-in.

"I should have known," he muttered. "Too tired indeed!"

Bruce bought a pair of snowshoes from a man in the parking lot, who was packing his car. He put them on, shouldered his skis, and began the trek to the top of the expert slope. It was slow, tedious going, filled with slipping, sliding, and snowdrifts that were waist high. A bit after midnight, Bruce finally stood atop the mountain. The sky was empty of clouds, and moonlight glowed on the snow: a Christmas card, a breathtakingly beautiful night, which Bruce noted only in passing. He had a mission. He shed the snowshoes, put on the skis, and stood poised at the top of the trail. Someone shouted at him—a night watchman, probably. Bruce turned his head in the direction of the shout, saluted with two fingers, and pushed off.

Ice flecks stung his cheeks, and his skis hissed on the powder as the trail rushed up to meet him, and he was enjoying himself until the world turned upside down . . .

The watchman had called the police, the police called the rescue patrol, and the rescue patrol, two medics, found Bruce at the bottom of a shallow gorge, unconscious, a bloody gash across his forehead, one of his skis lying in two pieces nearby, the other one canting his leg at an unnatural angle.

An hour later, Alfred entered the lodge's sick bay and found Bruce propped up in bed, his left leg encased in a cast, a white bandage across his forehead.

"I trust you had a pleasant rest," Alfred said.

"I'm afraid I don't have a comeback," Bruce said. "Head's pounding just a bit. Rain check?"

Alfred conferred with a doctor, who had been summoned from a nearby town, and learned that Bruce's leg was broken, but cleanly, and he had a slight concussion, a bad gash above his eyes that had required eleven stitches, and a lot of contusions. But, the doctor concluded, if Alfred wanted to take Bruce to Gotham, and could guarantee proper transportation, there should be no problem.

The "proper transportation" was a big, twin-rotor Sikorsky helicopter, which set down in a field next to Wayne Manor. Bruce slept in his own bed that night.

The bandage and cast came off, the contusions healed, and the Wayne family physician pronounced Bruce intact again.

Bruce never skied recreationally again, though he did do some cross-country skiing when he was at Rā's al Ghūl's monastery—he once went three days across snow-covered mountains without sleep—and on another occasion Rā's challenged him to ski down an almost vertical sheet of ice with jagged rocks at the bottom.

Bruce's interest eventually shifted to other athletics. He ordered a complete set of Olympic-grade gymnastics gear and spent most of a summer with an instructor learning how to use it. He had an Olympic-size pool dug behind the garden, and for several months swam laps before breakfast. He lifted weights. He ran. He cycled. But he wasn't good at everything. He was never able to get any arrow he loosed from a bow to go where it was aimed, and he was never better than a mediocre skater.

Rachel would sometimes join him at the manor to swim, or bounce around on the trampoline, or just hang out. Bruce seemed to enjoy these visits, but then, suddenly, he was seventeen and gone, without so much as a phone call.

The comings and goings continued until Bruce failed in an attempt to kill the man who had murdered his parents, had a final, ugly argument with Rachel and jumped aboard a rust bucket of a ship leaving Gotham Harbor. He was gone for years and when he at last reappeared, he was a different man. But only Alfred and Rachel could see what had changed . . .

TWO

With Batman came baggage. Most of it Bruce carried deep within himself, in the form of regrets, unanswered questions, and memories. During his pilgrimage from rich kid to vigilante, he'd gone many places, done many things, a lot of them ugly, one or two perhaps unforgivable. But he'd succeeded in what he wanted to accomplish; he'd learned, and equipped himself. He had been considering returning to Gotham City when a betrayal and a few other unforeseen circumstances put him in a filthy hole of a prison. There, he'd been offered a chance at freedom, and when he took it he found himself in yet another prison—a monastery, high in the Himalayas, where he became the acolyte of the most dangerous, and perhaps the most charismatic, man he had ever known.

Rā's al Ghūl. A man who hid both his brilliance and his malevolence behind another's identity until it pleased him to reveal himself. Bruce sometimes wondered if Rā's concealing himself behind another identity somehow lodged in his subconscious and, when the time came, prompted him to adopt a similar strategy.

Even now, Bruce could not decide whether Rā's was truly insane. Bruce knew that, by his own reckoning, Rā's was an altruist, a savior who would restore social and, more importantly, environmental order to a stricken planet. He would do this by means that would make Vlad the Impaler seem like a Sunday school teacher. He would eliminate most of the human beings on the Earth, and force the rest to live according to strict rules.

Rā's tolerated no disobedience, as Bruce learned when he ordered Bruce to execute a farmer who was guilty of theft. Bruce had refused, and in fleeing had set the monastery ablaze.

But before he had made his way down the mountain, he had stopped to rescue his mentor. That had been a mistake. Rā's had followed him to Gotham City and initiated a scheme to drive everyone there into hallucinating madness, and had partly succeeded.

You sometimes see them around town, Bruce thought. *The ones I couldn't save. The ones the doctors gave up on. Hollow-eyed, unaware of their surroundings . . . And those are the fortunate ones. The others . . . they're behind walls. They're fed, and sheltered, and clothed, and they scream and scream . . .*

It all came to an end on a train speeding toward the center of the city, when student and mentor confronted each other a final time

Some Gothamites, confused by conflicting reports, thought that the bat-man had caused the crash, others regarded him as a hero, and still others, perhaps the majority, doubted his existence.

When Alfred Pennyworth carried a tray of toast and coffee into Bruce Wayne's bedroom area, he found it empty, though the bed had been slept in—not always the case where Alfred's employer was concerned. He went down a long, empty corridor. Twice he had to flatten himself against a wall and inch past cartons that were still unpacked and were in the way. They had occupied this penthouse for less than a month and there was still work to do before Alfred could pronounce it livable.

Bruce Wayne was in an empty area performing one of the strange, dancelike routines Alfred knew was called a *kata*, and whose purpose was to train in Asian martial arts.

"Something Rā's al Ghūl taught you?" Alfred asked.

Bruce finished his exercise before answering: leapt and kicked simultaneously, and landed lightly on the balls of his feet. "Nope," he said. "Korean master. Last I heard, he was living in the Changansan mountains.

"Does this resumption of martial-arts practice indicate that you plan further nocturnal forays?"

"Not necessarily. I'm used to being in shape. Makes me feel good. I tried just sitting around yesterday, and it gave me the crawlies." Bruce looked at the tray. "That for me?"

Alfred nodded and put the tray on a windowsill. Bruce poured himself a cup of coffee.

"May I assume," Alfred asked, "that you're done with . . . busting heads?"

Bruce sipped his coffee. "I prefer to use the term 'vigorous persuasion.' What you're really asking is, am I done with Batman? I've given it a lot of thought these past few days and . . . no, I'm not."

"Rā's al Ghūl is dead."

"But there are others, close to home, who are just as dangerous. The job isn't done. For openers, there's the Maroni thing, the Rossi thing . . . I'm far from done . . ."

Alfred sighed. "I suppose I should begin to shop for some new equipment."

"For here? No, this room isn't nearly big enough. No room in the penthouse is."

"May I remind you that the cave beneath the mansion is . . ."

". . . Temporarily inaccessible, yes," finished Bruce. "That's something that has a high priority. What I have in mind will take a lot of hard work. You can expect a whopping Christmas bonus this year."

"Splendid. In the meantime, if you insist on continuing your nocturnal exploits, what will you do for a head-quarters? You can hardly wear the cape and mask and pass the doorman downstairs without being noticed."

"I think I've got that covered. I'll show you the place this afternoon. With a little elbow grease, we should be able to transform it into a bunker of sorts."

"My life," Alfred said, "becomes fuller and fuller."

Bruce finished his coffee as Alfred carried the empty tray to the kitchen.

THREE

It was what most of Gotham's citizens thought was a typical afternoon in the life of Bruce Wayne, playboy. A quick stop at a gallery opening, where he ignored the photographs on display but managed to get the phone number of the pretty receptionist. Lunch at a hip downtown bistro. A dash out to the country club, where he decided *not* to play golf but instead chased the female employees around with his clubs.

A trip back to central Gotham, waving at passersby from the window of his steel gray Lamborghini Murcielago.

Bruce drove the Lamborghini into the basement garage of the tall building he currently lived in, managed to knock over a Vespa scooter on the way to his parking slot, paid the Vespa's owner twice what it would cost to replace it, stashed the Lamborghini next to the other

Wayne vehicle, a Rolls-Royce, and rode the private elevator to his penthouse. There, he found that Alfred had company. He and Rachel Dawes were perched on stools in the kitchen, facing each other across a marble countertop, clutching mugs of what Bruce was sure was tea, deep in conversation. Both looked at him when he entered, and he called out a greeting.

"What brings you uptown?" he asked Rachel. "Or do you come *down*town . . . I can never remember where that office of yours is."

"*Up*town, as you well know."

"I thought you'd be busy . . . middle of a weekday and all."

"The case I was trying was plea bargained. No court time needed."

"Tell me . . . is that good or bad? This law stuff . . . so confusing."

"You don't have to do your act with me, Bruce. In fact, I wish you wouldn't. It annoys me."

"Sorry," Bruce said.

"I hope so."

"What are you and Alfred up to?"

"I came to see *you*."

"Okay. Shall we go into the living room?"

"Here is fine."

"More tea?" Alfred asked.

"That would be nice," Rachel said. Alfred refilled Rachel's cup and poured one for Bruce, then excused himself.

Bruce looked at Rachel across the counter. She had aged, but no one could complain about that. She had always been *cute*; now she was, by any reasonable criterion, *beautiful*. Beautiful and strong, and ferocious, compassionate, and brave.

"What you're doing is wrong," she said.

"Wrecking sports cars? Dating debutantes? What exactly . . ."

"Please, Bruce. No masquerade, not with me."

"Fair enough."

"There's something else. I'd like you to abandon your *other* masquerade."

"Which one would that be?"

"The Batman."

Bruce hesitated and sipped tea, then set down the mug. "Okay. What's your objection to . . . my new life?"

"I think you've begun to enjoy it. Too much. Oh, I'm sure you've constructed an elaborate rationalization—you're saving Gotham, et cetera et cetera et cetera . . . I'm afraid that sooner or later you'll become addicted to it, and that will cause you to cross the line."

"You're afraid I'll kill someone."

"Or cause someone to die . . . what you'd call 'collateral damage.' And you'll rationalize, tell yourself that it was necessary, it couldn't be helped, you were only following the dictates of the moment . . . Does that sound familiar to you?"

"No. Should it?"

"You should read history books. Then you might recognize some of the excuses war criminals offer."

"I'll be careful."

"You'll *try* to be careful, at least at first. But you'll be creating situations that you won't be able to control, situations in which people panic. I deal with cops and crooks all day, every day. I know what can happen to a person."

"With all due humility . . . I'm not just any *person*."

"You're richer than most. You're also incredibly intelligent, athletic, handsome, determined, motivated. But you swim in the same gene pool as we lesser mortals. You're fallible, and you're going to fail and someone *will* die. Then you'll either destroy yourself with remorse or become a homicidal sociopath. I don't know which would be worse."

"Sometimes violence is necessary."

"Yes. To save your life or someone else's life. But not as policy—you're proposing to use violence to solve enormously complex problems, and when has that ever worked? And it's been tried, oh, has it been tried! Remember the old definition of insanity—doing the same thing over and over and expecting a different result."

"Rachel, I promise you . . . I won't go off the deep end."

"I think you will."

"You know how much I respect your opinion, but this time, you're wrong."

"We'll see, then won't we?"

"I guess we will."

Alfred was feeling a bit guilty. He shouldn't have been listening to the private conversation, but if information passed between those two . . . he had to know what it was. And now he did, and now he was disturbed because he shared Rachel's misgivings. He wasn't as alarmed as she obviously was, but . . . he tended Bruce Wayne's wounds, always trying to joke about them to lighten the moment, and he'd observed the subtle changes in Bruce since his return from his adventures abroad and his time with Rā's al Ghūl. Of course, Bruce was no longer the bright, charming child he'd been when he and Alfred met and, people did change as they age; perhaps the traits Alfred was observing were simply the result of Bruce getting older. But he still couldn't help being bothered.

When she got up to leave, he escorted Rachel to the door, told her that he would see her soon, and went to see how Bruce was enjoying his tea.

The Joker saw the bus, about a block away, and—was this great or what?—an old lady waiting near the curb. It would be a matter of perfect timing, but the Joker loved that kind of challenge. He stood directly behind the old lady. The bus came closer, closer, just a few feet away . . .

The Joker let it pass.

Then he tapped the old lady on the shoulder and handed her a hundred-dollar bill.

FOUR

Midafternoon, Friday, downtown Gotham City. North Julius Street, on the edge of the financial district. Noise and confusion. Blaring horns and rumbling engines and sunlight glaring on thousands of panes of glass. A thin blue haze of exhaust fumes hanging in the air.

Above it all, on the fourteenth floor of a skyscraper still under construction, two men wearing clown masks, with weapons and tools strapped to their bodies, were standing in a vacant loft facing a ten-foot-tall window. The first of the men, whose code name was Dopey, aimed upward, fired a silenced automatic pistol at the glass, and watched shards of it fall to the floor. The second man, code named Happy, stepped to the now empty window frame and lifted what looked like a spear gun to his shoulder, aimed, squeezed the trigger, and a hook trailing a length of cable, hissed across the street and buried itself in the wall of another building. Dopey secured his end of the cable to a naked I-beam and nodded to his partner. Happy hooked a bag to the cable and sent it across the emptiness. A moment later, Happy and Dopey followed the bag, dangling from wheeled devices that fit over the line. If anyone happened to look up and see them . . . *Hey, this is Gotham City, whack-job central. Just another pair of loonies doing something loony, and if it's interesting, maybe it'll be on the eleven o'clock news . . .*

Below, and three blocks away, a black SUV with dark-tinted windows and out-of-state license plates sped between two school buses and jerked to a stop at an intersection. The front passenger door opened, and a tall man wearing coveralls dashed from a doorway and climbed into the vehicle. Once inside, he pulled a clown mask from his pocket, pulled it on, and turned in his seat to face another clown, code named Bozo, in the driver's seat. "Three of a kind. Let's do this," he said, now going by the name Grumpy.

The man in the backseat, code named Chuckles, looked up from loading a compact submachine gun, and said, "That's it? Three guys?"

Grumpy said, "There are two on the roof. Every guy is an extra share. Five shares is plenty."

Chuckles said, "*Six* shares. Don't forget the guy who planned the job."

Grumpy said, "Yeah? If he thinks he can sit it out and still take a slice then I get why they call him the Joker."

On the rooftop, Dopey and Happy pried open an access panel. Happy paused and stared at Dopey. "Why do they call him the Joker?"

"I heard it's 'cause he wears makeup," Chuckles said, pulling out a thick bundle of blue CAT5 cables. "To scare people. War paint."

Back on the street, Bozo guided the SUV to a metered parking spot in front of the bank. He switched off the engine and, without bothering to feed the meter, went into the bank. Grumpy, Bozo, and Chuckles carried assault rifles; they carried several empty duffel bags as well. Once inside, Grumpy fired a burst into the ceiling as Chuckles hit the security guard on the head with the butt of his weapon, and Bozo closed the door and lowered the blinds.

Grumpy fired another burst, and yelled, "Everybody down on the floor—*now!*" Customers and employees alike dropped to their hands and knees, then to their bellies. One of the senior tellers managed to press a silent-alarm button as she went down. Fifteen floors above her, on the roof, Dopey stared down at a palm-sized electronic device and heard a faint *ping*.

"What's that?" Happy asked.

"Here comes the silent alarm, just like we figured," Dopey said. "And there it goes. Funny thing is, it didn't dial out to the cops. It was trying to reach a private number."

Behind him, Happy raised his gun and fired his silenced automatic into the back of Dopey's head. As Dopey slumped to the roof dead, Happy picked up his bag. He took from it an old-fashioned crowbar and went to work on the roof access door. In less than a minute, he had it wrenched open and was running down a steep flight of steps, lit only by red bulbs on each landing. When he reached the bottom, he opened a door marked EXIT and was standing in front of a shiny steel vault.

In the bank proper, Bozo and Grumpy were moving down a line of customers and tellers, who stood along one wall. Bozo handed each a hand grenade and Grumpy followed, pulling the pins. The hostages gripped the grenades in both hands, holding the tops to prevent the grenades from exploding.

"We don't want you doing anything with your hands other than holding on for dear life," Grumpy told the hostages.

Then there was a loud *bang* and the third robber, Chuckles, fell backward, his mask and the front of his jacket shredded, dead.

The bank manager, wearing an impeccably tailored brown suit and holding a shotgun, stepped from his office and fired again. The hostages, clutching their grenades, scurried along the floor seeking cover. Grumpy and Bozo both fired blindly in the general direction of the manager with the shotgun as they dived behind a desk.

"What's he got, a five-shot?" Grumpy asked.

Bozo nodded.

"He's got three left?"

Bozo raised two fingers.

Grumpy edged his gun around the corner of the desk and squeezed off a single shot. The bank manager fired twice. Grumpy looked at Bozo, who nodded.

Grumpy stood and aimed his gun over the desktop. The bank manager fired again and a hail of buckshot clipped Grumpy's shoulder. He fell behind the desk and the manager moved forward, pulling fresh shells from his pocket. Bozo stood from behind the desk and shot the manager in the chest.

Grumpy had pulled aside the flaps of his shirt and jacket over the place where the buckshot had struck him and was peering down at his wound. He rubbed some blood away with the palm of his hand and looked more closely. The damage was only superficial.

Leaning on the desk, he stood and turned to Bozo. "Where'd you learn to count?"

Bozo ignored him and started loading fresh shells into his shotgun.

"You have any idea who you're stealing from?" the bank manager whispered. "You and your friends are *dead*."

Happy clamped a drill to the vault and pressed a button. With a high whine, the drill blade bit into the metal and—

He found himself on the floor, dazed and shaking. It took him a few moments to realize that he'd been hit by electricity, a *lot* of electricity. They wired the *vault*?

He pulled his sneakers off, put them on his hands and, bracing himself on a wall, approached the vault once more. With a lot of fumbling and repositioning, he was able to operate the drill, the sneakers protecting him from the high voltage.

Grumpy entered the chamber from a side door. Happy glanced at him, and said, "They wired this thing up with—I dunno, maybe five thousand volts. What kind of bank does that?"

"A mob bank," Grumpy said. "I guess the Joker's as crazy as they say."

Happy shrugged. The noise of the drill changed from a whine to a grinding sound. "We're almost home," Happy said.

He grabbed the large wheel and spun it.

"Where's the alarm guy?" Grumpy asked.

The wheel stopped spinning. Happy pulled on it, and the vault swung open. "Boss told me that when the guy was done I should take him out. One less share."

"Funny," Grumpy said. "He told me something similar."

Happy grabbed for the pistol shoved into his belt at the small of his back as he whirled to face Grumpy, but he was too late. Grumpy fired a burst from his assault rifle and, after a moment, stepped over Happy's body and into the vault.

He stopped and stared at the mountain of cash at least eight feet tall.

Ten minutes later, he emerged into the bank burdened by several bulging duffel bags. He dropped them at Bozo's feet and laughed.

"C'mon," he said. "There's a lot to carry."

The hostages, clutching their grenades, watched as the robbers disappeared into the vault. Some of them glanced nervously at their neighbors, others stared at nothing in particular, while still others had their eyes squeezed shut, their lips moving silently.

Grumpy and Bozo reappeared, each burdened with several stuffed duffel bags. Grumpy dropped his bags onto the floor next to the first batch and said, "If this guy was so smart, he would have had us bring a bigger car."

Then he jammed his pistol into Bozo's back and took his weapon. "I'm betting the Joker told you to kill me soon as we loaded the cash."

Bozo shook his head. "No. I kill the bus driver."

"Bus driver? What bus—"

Bozo glanced at the nearest window and jumped back. The rear end of a yellow school bus smashed through the window, sending a shower of glass into the room and slamming Grumpy into the tellers' cage. Bozo snatched up Grumpy's fallen weapon and turned to face the bus. Another clown opened the bus's rear door, and Bozo shot him dead.

Sirens began to wail in the distance.

Bozo began loading the duffel bags into the bus.

The bank manager still lay where he'd fallen, his right hand splayed over his wound, his head raised to stare at Bozo. "Think you're smart, huh?" he wheezed. "Well, the guy who hired you'll just do the same to you. Sure he will. Criminals in this town used to believe in things."

Bozo stepped over to where the man lay and crouched beside him.

The man stared up at Bozo. "Honor. Respect. What do you beli—"

Bozo jammed a grenade with a purple thread knotted around the pin into the man's mouth.

"I believe," Bozo said, "that what doesn't kill you—"

Bozo yanked off his mask. The manager's eyes widened. He was looking at another clown face, one far more disturbing than any of the masks: white skin, green hair, a mouth horribly scarred beneath a red slash of makeup.

"—simply makes you *stranger*," the Joker concluded.

The scarred clown rose and strolled toward the bus, the thread attached to the grenade unraveling from the purple lining of his jacket. He climbed into the bus and shut the rear door, trapping the purple thread.

A moment later, the bus engine grumbled, and the bus jerked over the sidewalk and into the street.

The purple thread yanked the pin from the grenade in the bank manager's mouth.

Hostages screamed.

The grenade hissed and began spewing red smoke, but it did not explode.

A block away, a line of school buses left the curb in front of the Ferguson Middle School and edged into the traffic stream. A final bus, which came from the direction of the bank, joined them as five police cars, sirens screaming, sped past them on the opposite side of the street.

FIVE

The Chechen sipped fine wine, looked across the dance floor at a fine woman, and listened to music which was not fine, but popular here in his new country, the United States of America.

Some said he was lucky, this native of Chechnya, very lucky indeed not to be dead or eating moldy bread in some godforsaken prison cell. The Chechen knew luck had nothing to do with it. He was tough, he was as smart as he had to be, and he did not care about anyone or anything except his own well-being, and that made him invulnerable.

He was just a boy when Chechnya broke away from Russia in the early 90s, nothing but fuzz on his cheeks, but already he knew opportunity when he saw it, already he was realizing that the chaos that gripped his small nation could be turned to his advantage. So he got some guns, a lot of guns, abandoned by fleeing Russian troops, and the guns enabled him to get followers, and the followers and the guns together enabled him to get more guns and more followers . . . For a while, he was one of the most feared and powerful men in his region, and by then he had something more than fuzz on his cheeks, but not *much* more. In the United States, he would not have been able to vote yet; in his country, he was a dominator. He was sure that nothing could stop him. But something did. The damned Russian army—*that* stopped him. The Communists were gone, or temporarily in hiding, but the politicians and generals—were they about to let tiny Chechnya make a mockery of the mother country? No. And so tiny Chechnya was reinvaded, and this time, the Russians were victorious.

That was fine with him. Russians the bosses? Deal with them. Not selling them guns and rockets, perhaps—they seemed to have plenty of guns and rockets. But there were other things. Drugs? Yes, people always wanted drugs, and as long as the authorities were so stupid as to outlaw drugs, money could be made from them.

By now, he despised the name he was born with because it reminded him of his parents, a pair of weaklings, a pair of fools who deserved the squalor they lived in, but he was not good at things requiring imagination, things such as thinking of a new name. Boris? Too

Russian. Peter? Too Christian. In the end, he told people to call him "the Chechen."

He went into the business of supplying drugs to Russian troops, both officers and enlisted men but mostly officers because they had more money. Then something happened. He never learned exactly what it was, but one night, sitting in the rear seat of his car as one of his hirelings delivered cocaine to a major general, he saw police emerge from a van and storm into the major general's quarters. There were shots. Police cars blocked both ends of the street. The windshield of the Chechen's car shattered and his driver's head fell back, a widening splotch of blood on his forehead. The Chechen got a machine pistol from under the seat, rolled out the car door and, bent over, staying low, ran for a narrow passageway between two houses. He heard yelling and footfalls behind him. When he reached the end of the passageway, he turned around and sprayed bullets at the policemen who were chasing him. There were four of them and they all fell, and he ran again. He found a culvert beneath a roadway and squeezed into it, gasping, spit running down his chin.

He waited and listened. There was the distant rumble of traffic, but no footfalls, no sirens. He stayed in the culvert for an hour, waiting, listening. Finally, he climbed out and hiked to a place he knew near an airfield. He used the cash in his pockets to obtain use of a computer and the computer to access bank accounts in the Bahamas. He used that cash to bribe and obtain a private aircraft, and within a week he was comfortably ensconced in a luxury hotel in Mexico City. The Russians, he was pretty sure, would not seek him in Mexico, and by the time they realized that he might have gone there, he would have vanished again.

What next? He liked the drug trade, liked feeling superior to the weaklings who were his customers, liked the money. And he was close to the United States. But where in the United States? New York, Chicago, Miami, both ends of California, St. Louis—it would be difficult to establish himself in places like those because businessmen such as he already had both monopolies and small armies of enforcers, and his own army was gone, its members either dead or behind bars. But this Gotham City he had heard of? From what he already knew and was able to learn through telephone calls, Gotham City had been a paradise of corruption and a marketplace for his kind of goods. The rumor was, the situation in Gotham was even worse than usual. Something big had happened, something nobody could quite explain: escaped maniacs, exploding manholes, a commuter train that crashed into a street and burst into flames, ordinary citizens rampaging, insane . . . and a giant bat that was part human. That last, the bat—it had to be something made up, perhaps to sell newspapers. The Chechen did not believe in human bats. But the rest was true, at least most of it. There were pictures and eyewitness accounts.

The whole story could be a hoax, perpetrated by the government, but the Chechen did not think so, because there was no profit to be made from such lies.

If the television reporters were to be believed, the situation in Gotham City had improved, but it was still largely chaos. Perhaps it was like his country after the Russians had fled? That would be made to order for him. That would be perfect.

The man to see, the boss of bosses, was named Salvatore Maroni. The Chechen would have to deal with him. But first, he would have to prove himself. He found an enclave of refugees from his part of the world in a small city near Gotham, called Blüdhaven, armed them and led them in a successful raid on the biggest local dealer. News media called the event a "massacre," and for once, the label was accurate. No survivors, and a row of storefronts in downtown Blüdhaven in flames. The Chechen now owned the Blüdhaven drug trade. Maroni did what he would have done, and got in touch. Discussions were held, deals made, and in the end, Sal Maroni and the Chechen were co-operators, and virtually every junkie in both Bludhaven and Gotham City were clients.

The Chechen had always planned to kill Maroni as soon as it was convenient, but he found that their informal partnership was useful. As the Americans would say, they had each other's back. Perhaps later, when he understood America better, the Chechen would kill Maroni, but for the time being, and for the foreseeable future, they were allies. Maroni introduced him to others of what the press called "the underworld" and, again, deals were made and everyone profited.

The Chechen bought himself a nice house in a Gotham suburb, one with a high fence and living quarters for his bodyguards and large, luxurious kennels for his dogs. The rottweilers were the animals he favored, big and nasty and ferocious, like himself. Next, he sought recreation. None of the nightspots were to his liking, nothing like the clubs he'd seen in old Hollywood movies, except for the one owned by Maroni, and the Chechen didn't want to get *too* close to his partner because . . . well, perhaps Maroni planned to kill *him*—it was surely possible—and if he allowed himself to be distracted by the pleasures of a nightclub, the killing would be easy, and that was to say nothing of poison in the food and drink. The Chechen's solution was the obvious one, a nightclub of his own, and it proved to be an *excellent* solution.

His nightclub was where he preferred to do business, surrounded by his rottweilers, bodyguards, and lady friends, and it was in his nightclub that he met with a small time dealer named Burton. It was a Tuesday night, not a big night in the nightclub business; there was only one couple on the dance floor, a man with white hair and a woman who looked to be in her late teens, and no one at the bar. Burton came in with his two bodyguards who took up stations opposite the Chechen's bodyguards and the two sets of men glared at each other, hands near the lapels of their jackets, while their bosses sat in a circular banquette upholstered in rhinoceros hide and conferred.

Burton had news: he had discovered a new source of product he felt the Chechen should know about. A highly trained man with doctorates in both chemistry and medicine who was able to synthesize a product that would put the average user into orbit.

"This man has name?" the Chechen asked.

"Most people do," Burton said. "This guy has two. The one he was born with is Jonathan Crane—"

"Sounds like sissy," the Chechen said.

"—but the one he likes to use is the Scarecrow."

"Sounds like sissy at costume party. Why we can trust him?"

"He has this little problem with the cops. They'd like to hang his ass on a flagpole. You maybe heard about what happened in Gotham last year? Lotta people going nuts? Crane was part'a the reason. Nobody knows all that happened, but Crane was in on it. We give him a place to work, a cut of the profit, he delivers us the goods, and we don't haveta worry about foreign suppliers. Nice little domestic operation. Good for us, good for America."

"You vouch for him?"

"I ain't gonna go that far. What I'm saying is, he's a solution to a problem. He stops being a solution, he ain't bulletproof, know what I'm saying? You in or out?"

"In. What you need from me?"

"Right now, money. A couple days, I'll call, set up a meet with you and Crane."

"Deal." The Chechen leaned back and almost smiled. "You hungry? Thirsty? You want drink? Food—steak?"

"In *your* place? Do you think I'm crazy?"

SIX

Rupert Casterbaugh was what some people, the charitable ones, would have once called a "remittance man." Others, less charitable, might have used words like "wastrel," "lay about," "worthless waste of protoplasm." He had no job, no relationships, no prospects and, truth to tell, no idea how he landed in Gotham City. But land there he did, in a studio apartment in an expensive building. This gave him a fixed address, a place for his mother to send a monthly check that paid the rent on the studio and Rupert's other, quite modest, living expenses, and his single *major* need, the stuff he absolutely could not live without: drugs. Rupert Casterbaugh was an addict—a *junkie,* to the uncharitable and a "bright young man with a problem" to his mother—and he could and did easily blow a hundred thousand a year feeding his habit.

He was nice. Polite, well-spoken, even funny. The few women who drifted in and out of his life found him sad and in profound psychological pain, but they couldn't help him, and neither could the platoon of therapists his mother employed from time to time. So he wandered from city to city, country to country, befogged and lonely and not caring. Gotham City? Why not? It was as good a place as any, and a man he'd met in Tangiers had set him up with a supplier, which meant that Rupert would not lack for life's necessities once there.

The first meeting between merchant and customer was the usual—furtive and fast. But the drug, whatever it was—a white powder—the drug was way better than anything he'd ever tried, and he didn't know why. A lot of his drug use was about, at first, killing pain and later about simply quelling the need. But *this* . . . It was always impossible to convey to lucky nonaddicts—and he admitted that they *were* lucky—why putting the liquid into a vein or sniffing the powder or puffing the pipe was happy-making. But *this* . . . he couldn't explain it even to himself!

When the high was done, he became worried that something that powerful must have damaged his body somehow. But he could detect no new problems. He'd been undernourished for years, and pale, and a bit yellowish in certain light, and he still had all those symptoms. But no new ones. Oh, he desperately wanted some more of the white powder, but after a high, he *always* wanted and needed more. Maybe the wanting and the need were a bit more intense, but hey . . . small price to pay, right?

The second transaction was better than the first—more civilized, more friendly. The merchant came to Rupert's apartment: no meetings on dark street corners, parks, bars. No, a call from the doorman, a doorbell ring, and in came a pleasant-looking fellow in his early 30s who introduced himself as Crane. They shook hands and Crane asked if he might trouble Rupert for a glass of water. Water was all Rupert could supply because, as usual, his pantries and refrigerator were empty, but that was okay—water was all Crane wanted, really.

Rupert handed Crane a wad of bills, which Crane did not bother to count—classy!—and received in return a baggie with a few ounces of white powder visible through the plastic.

"Try it," Crane suggested.

Rupert snorted directly from the bag . . . and looked up to see Crane with a crude burlap mask over his head.

Why was he screaming? And why was Crane putting tape over his mouth?

He slid over an edge, and drowning or burning or being torn apart would be better than this namelessness and *no no no no no no no no no . . .*

Rupert was dead. Crane used a cell phone to call for

help in removing the body. "I want to examine it more closely," he told somebody.

The so-called *authorities* would have said that Jonathan Crane wasn't qualified to conduct an autopsy since his license had been revoked after his activities as the Scarecrow became known. He knew this because the information appeared in the last paragraph of a story in the *Gotham Times* about the chaos in Gotham City that ended, somehow, when a commuter train car exploded. Crane had fled Arkham Asylum by then. He was in hiding and not, himself, at all certain what had happened after he'd been thwarted by that insane meddler in the bat costume; that was why he was bothering to read news reports.

Crane wondered exactly where he would examine Rupert's body and, more particularly, Rupert's brain. It would have to be a place with plenty of light and . . . yes, plenty of running water. Autopsies could be messy. If he were still in residence at Arkham, he would have no problem. Although the asylum was, in most ways, a bit old-fashioned, even Gothic, someone somewhere along the way had equipped it with a first-rate morgue.

That morgue was just one of the reasons Crane had found a home at Arkham. He'd found the institution's relaxed attitude toward the silly rules of ethical practice congenial, not like his previous place of employment. Not that rules didn't have their place, but they were for those of limited intellect who needed them, and Jonathan Crane did *not* need them because he had known from an early age that his intellect was anything but limited. He was a visionary. He was a *genius*. To hamper him in any way was to do a disservice to mankind.

The fossils he'd associated with earlier in his career were too dense, too involved in "procedure," to comprehend the benefits Crane's work could eventually confer on the herd known as humanity. Not that anyone doubted his brilliance. He had, after all, gotten his doctorate in psychology as the absurdly early age of twenty-one, after submitting a thesis on the etiology of the fear reflex in higher mammals, including *homo sapiens*. His dissertation committee called the paper "brilliant," "groundbreaking," "as important in its way as anything Freud ever wrote." Jonathan Crane, now *Doctor* Jonathan Crane, was hired by Gotham University, the same university that had given him his degree, and ensconced in the psychology department where many predicted for him a long and distinguished career. Many, but not all. He did have a habit of annoying his colleagues, mostly by showing open contempt for achievements, ambitions and, occasionally, even their physical appearances. And he generally described his students as "dumber than pond scum." But he *was* a professor, and weren't professors *supposed* to be eccentric? For a while, Dr. Crane's bad manners merely enhanced his mystique—for he did have a mystique, woven from his intelligence, youth and, yes, personal beauty. He was as handsome as he was smart, and he knew it—and let everyone else *know* he knew it.

Then, the rumors began. Only Dr. Crane and five of his grad students knew they were more than rumors, these hushed tales of illicit experiments. Some said it was just a retelling of what had happened to Richard Alport and Timothy Leary at Harvard in the sixties: certain favored youngsters fed illegal drugs by a charismatic teacher. They stopped being rumors and became facts when one of Dr. Crane's students ran through the a plate-glass window of a department store on Christmas Eve and tried to dismember the Santa Claus mannequin who was *ho, ho, ho*ing to a bunch of mannequin elves. At the emergency room, she told the admitting nurse that she was only "trying to face" her fears. Further questioning revealed her connection to Dr. Crane; she had taken a shot of what Dr. Crane called a "party potion" an hour before her collision with Santa.

That was the beginning of the end of Dr. Crane's academic career. His situation got worse, and quickly. One of the other professors, a man Dr. Crane had treated with particular scorn, had been quietly investigating Crane's vaunted doctoral thesis and discovered that the research was either plagiarized or faked. Crane was called before a meeting of the university staff and asked for an explanation. He had one: he said that he *knew* his conclusions were valid because his insight was so much deeper than that of his inquisitors and had chosen not to waste his valuable time doing the dreary, boring chores that would constitute "proof." Most of the faculty wanted to fire him immediately and as publicly as possible. They were overruled by the school's president, Dr. Titus V. Blaney, and some of them guessed why. Dr. Blaney, whose own doctorate was in psychology, had been especially voluble in praising young Crane, and had personally vouched for the dissertation. "I'd stake my reputation on this young wizard's achievement," he had told the *Gotham Times*. In making this statement, he *had*, in fact, staked his reputation on Crane, who now appeared to be more than an egotistical braggart; he was a *fraudulent* egotistical braggart. Not good for the university, not good for the fundraising effort and the repute of the president. A compromise was reached: Crane was quietly dismissed at the end of the semester. The public relations office distributed a press release stating that Dr. Crane was reluctantly leaving his post to pursue other opportunities, including research in the private sector.

Members of the academic community knew the real story, of course. All the men and women who had been mocked by Jonathan Crane fired up their computers and spread the word, gleefully. Apparently, the doctors at Arkham Asylum didn't get the bad news about Dr. Crane. They hired him as chief of research and gave him license to experiment on the inmates. There, at Arkham, he had discovered that putting on a mask furthered those experiments, and gradually he developed an alter ego he called "the Scarecrow." By then, some fellow psychologists might have said that Crane, himself, was insane.

Crane was willing to admit the possibility that he was, by clinical standards, unbalanced to the point of insanity. But what he was not ready to admit was that those standards, while relevant to most humans, were not relevant to him. He vowed to leave his brain to science when he died because he knew that he was extraordinary, and his immense gifts probably originated in his brain. In the meantime . . . he was content to be Arkham Asylum's resident genius. He was sure that in five years, maybe less, he would arrive at a grand theory, one that would prove that fear was the basis for all of humanity's errors and that he could *cure* fear and thus usher mankind into a true Garden of Eden, one that would endure until the sun cooled. Crane envisioned himself as the benevolent ruler of the entire planet once the fear-induced borders and barriers had been eradicated and the Earth became, truly, a brave new world. He would begin by learning to induce fear and with the knowledge he gained would learn to inoculate against it. He just needed a little more time.

Then everything was ruined. A foreigner who called himself Rā's al Ghūl offered Crane a chance to test his drug on a huge cross section of the human species—the entire population of Gotham City, as a matter of fact—and Crane thought he had found his own particular paradise. By observing the effects of his experiment on *millions* of diverse people, he could shave years from his time line! He eagerly accepted the foreigner's offer. And then the Batman came, the meddling, obtuse Batman, and wreaked havoc: destroyed his facility at the asylum, compromised his test subjects, ruined most of the work he was doing in the city at large—only a few thousand Gothamites were affected by his drug, not the millions he needed to confirm his hypotheses—and, worst of all, this masked vigilante drove Jonathan from his comfortable existence to poverty and degradation. He was forced to abandon his cozy apartment in Gotham Heights and the asylum that he'd spent months investing in and . . . hide. That's what he did—hide.

First, he had to flee from Arkham, when the damage had become undeniable, the Batman-wrought debacle a stark and leering fact. Fortunately, the streets around the asylum were dark and there was a lot of confusion, so Crane was able to leave the asylum unnoticed. He had no plan, beyond somehow getting across the river to the main part of the city and from there to . . . somewhere. Two policemen, hands on their holstered weapons, passed near him and Crane pressed himself against a wall, shrouded in darkness. He heard one of the officers say what sounded like his name and realized, with a jolt of pain, that they, the authorities, the police, the FBI for all he knew, were seeking him. Were looking for whom? For Jonathan Crane! And if he became someone else, he would, it stood to reason, be safe. He patted his clothing and found what he sought stuffed into a coat pocket. The mask, the scarecrow mask he used as a tool in psychotherapy. He pulled it on over his head and—

Felt a shift deep inside himself. Felt *Jonathan Crane* shrink and diminish and almost vanish entirely. Felt another *self* swell within him, fill him, seize him. And who was this newcomer? Why, the *Scarecrow*, of course. He stood still, alone in the dark, his senses alive and tingling. Then he heard a sound, a *clop clop*, the sound of hooves on the ancient cobblestones, and saw a policeman riding a brown horse round a corner, barely visible in the moonlight, and stop not ten feet from him. Crane crouched . . . No, not Crane—*Scarecrow* crouched, hoping to make himself less likely to be seen. For a moment, he lost his balance and thrust out an arm, hoping to right himself. His hand fell on something round and hard and cold: a paving stone, somehow loosened from the street. The Scarecrow lifted it, weighed it, liking the solidity and heft.

The policeman was leaning down, patting his horse's flanks. Looking for something? A scratch, some sort of injury?

The Scarecrow became the kind of being Jonathan Crane had never been, a creature of pure action. He stood and sprang and struck the policeman with the stone, and after the policeman's cap had fallen off, struck again and yet again. The policeman slumped, but did not fall completely off his mount; his boot was caught in the stirrup, leaving only half of him on the street.

The Scarecrow leapt over the animal's rump and into the saddle. Could a horse swim across the river? If so, the Scarecrow's troubles were as good as gone. All he had to do was ride the horse across the water, to downtown Gotham City, and perhaps on to an airport or the big railroad station. By dawn, he could be a thousand miles away.

But he had a new problem. There were no pedals to push, no gearshifts. He remembered seeing actors in cowboy movies halt horses by pulling on those straps—the *reins*? But how did one make a horse go?

"Giddyap," he said.

The horse began to move, slowly, dragging the policeman's body.

"Faster," the Scarecrow said.

The horse ignored him. But at least it was moving. Then it stopped. The street was blocked by about a dozen men and women. In the dim glow of the moon, now blurred with a thick fog, the Scarecrow could see that the people in front of him were all wearing the orange jumpsuits of Arkham Asylum inmates. Some sat, some stood motionless, others walked in tight circles.

"Out of the way," the Scarecrow shouted.

"Where should we go?" an inmate asked.

The Scarecrow considered: could Jonathan Crane's former patients possibly be of any use? Perhaps.

"Follow me," he said to the group, and to the horse: "Giddyap."

The horse remained motionless.

"Hit 'im with your heels," an inmate suggested.

The Scarecrow did, and the horse began to trot, dragging the dead cop and followed by a small troupe of inmates. Ahead and to his right, the Scarecrow saw someone he recognized, even in the dim light, a woman he had dealt with at the asylum. Rachel Dawes. She was standing next to a child.

"Dr. Crane?" she shouted.

How *dare* she! How dare she call him by his *old* name!

"Not Crane," he screamed. *"Scarecrow!"*

The woman, the insolent Dawes person, grabbed the child and began to run. The Scarecrow struck his heels against the horse and followed her. She stumbled but continued running. She turned into an alley and stopped. Blank wall. A dead end. She was trapped.

The Scarecrow pulled on the reins and the horse stopped. Several of the inmates who had been trotting behind the animal also stopped and crowded around it.

"Let me help you," the Scarecrow said, his voice muffled by the mask.

Rachel pulled the boy behind her and reached into her shoulder bag.

The horse reared back, front hooves pawing the air.

"Try shock therapy," Rachel said, and pulled a Taser from her bag. She shot it at Crane and the barbs caught in the sacking of his mask. Electrical sparks arced across Crane's face. He screamed and went limp. The horse whinnied and galloped back the way it had come.

The inmates scattered.

Scarecrow didn't know when he fell off the horse or how long he had lain on the cobblestones. When he opened his eyes, the fog had thickened even more, and the moon was only the faintest of blurs. Leaning against the pavement, he got to his feet and wobbled for a moment. Where to go? Not the asylum. The place would be full of police and, worse, much worse, the Batman might still be there somewhere. No, the asylum was out. But where else? His original destination had been the riverfront, and that might yet be a good idea. Maybe he could find a boat, or hire someone to ferry him across.

A new problem: where was the river? His fall had completely disoriented him and the thick fog hid landmarks, anything familiar to him. He had to do something, though, so he began walking, simply walking.

A voice from behind: "Doc? That you, Dr. Crane?"

No! he wanted to scream. *I'm Scarecrow!*

But was he? No, not exactly. He was *both* the Scarecrow and Jonathan Crane right now, which was actually nice. The ruck of humanity had only a single identity; it was fitting that a superior man have more than one. He pulled off the burlap mask and became Crane again.

"Yes, it's Crane," he called back to the voice.

A silhouette appeared in the fog, a dark shape in the mist, and approached. When it was only a few feet away, Jonathan could see the orange jumpsuit and recognize the smudgy face: a patient named Hooper.

"I come back to see if you was okay," Hooper said. "I feel bad about leaving you. You was always nice to me."

Was I? I don't remember. What did I treat him for?

"That's kind of you," Crane said.

"Can I do something for you?"

"You wouldn't have someplace I could stay for a few days?"

"Sure, that's where I was headed. My uncle's got a garage down by the river. Won't be fancy, but it'll be warm."

"Lead on," Crane said.

For the next fifteen minutes, Crane was utterly lost. He had no idea where he was. All he could do was follow Hooper through the narrow, winding streets, and hope for the best. And also hope that Hooper wasn't a homicidal maniac. Then he heard the lapping of water, and Hooper stopped in front of a two-story building with a sign that Crane couldn't see clearly enough to read. It was hanging over a door wide enough to accommodate two cars. Hooper knocked on a smaller door, waited, and when it opened said, "Hello, Uncle Joe."

The door opened wider, and Crane followed Hooper inside, into a garage much larger than Crane had thought. Two cars were partially disassembled, and a third was stripped down to the chassis. There were tools scattered on the greasy floor, stacks of tires and workbenches along the walls. No windows. No amenities. A stench that made Crane want to gag.

Hooper gestured to a thin, bald man, wearing a tank top and a torn, rolled-down grease-stained gray jumpsuit, who needed a shave and a bath and was holding a pistol against his leg. "Dr. Crane, this's my uncle. Uncle Joe, this's Dr. Crane."

"Yeah," Uncle Joe said. He did not offer to shake hands, which was fine with Crane.

"Pleased to meet you," Crane said.

"No you ain't," the uncle said to Crane. And to Hooper: "They let you go or you run?"

"We ran."

"Him, too?"

"I'm a fugitive, just like your nephew," Crane said.

"You better be. If you ain't, I'll kill you."

"We need a place to stay till things cool down," Hooper said.

"What I figured," the uncle said. "Okay, you're family. You can stay out back."

"Out back" was a toolshed. There was a canvas army cot, two blankets, a sleeping bag, a hot plate, an electric space heater, and hundreds of bits of scrap: wire, metal, paper, cardboard, wooden boards, irregular chunks of aluminum siding.

"You're the guest," Hooper said. "You take the cot."

Hooper, still wearing his Arkham jumpsuit, climbed into the sleeping bag, and curled into a fetal position. Crane lay on the cot, pulled one of the tattered blankets over himself, and did not sleep—did not dare to sleep, with a possible mad man snoring loud enough to rattle windows a few feet away and a tide of god-awful stink washing over him.

The next morning, Crane followed Hooper into the garage, where, standing at a workbench, they ate cold cereal and drank instant coffee. The chassis and one of the partially stripped cars were gone, and two men who did not acknowledge Crane's presence were using torches and saws on an SUV. The screech of the saws was horrendous, and the stench had not abated. Hooper did not seem to mind any of it.

There was a plastic radio on a shelf above the bench, cracked and yellowing. Crane reached to it, then hesitated and asked Hooper, "May I?"

Hooper nodded.

The sound quality of the radio was no better than its

casing, full of static, but Crane could hear enough to know he had tuned into the local all-news station. He heard his own name and moved his ear closer to the speaker.

" . . . *among the missing, Dr. Jonathan Crane, who is believed to have perished in the chaos at the asylum . . .*"

For a moment, he was outraged: *Dead? Me? I'm not dead!* But then he smiled. If he were dead, they wouldn't be looking for him. Being dead might afford him great freedom.

He smelled Hooper's uncle before he turned to greet the old man. "Good morning."

"No it ain't. The boy says you're some kinda doctor."

"True."

"You know anything about drugs?"

Crane's suspicions were confirmed: he was in the midst of an illegal enterprise and speaking to a criminal. Better and better.

"As a matter of fact, I know most of what there *is* to know about drugs."

"Yeah? I got some contacts be happy to hear that. If it's true. If it ain't, they'll kill you. Or I will."

"I'd like to meet them."

"It can happen."

And it did, but not immediately. Gotham City was still trying to recover from . . . from whatever it had been that drove all those people around the bend. For the next two days, the bridges and tunnels were closed except to police and emergency vehicles, and public transportation did not exist. But by the end of the week, what might have passed for normality was restored, and the city resumed most of its routines.

Hooper's uncle drove Crane into Gotham City to a dimly lit restaurant near the piers. There, they met two men in suits and dark glasses and discussed illegal drugs. Crane had a sense that he was not talking to anyone significant in the underworld hierarchy, but that did not bother him. These oafs would do. The meeting ended with Crane giving the men a long shopping list—things he needed to synthesize several of the more popular narcotics. Nobody shook hands.

The next morning, a blue van arrived at the uncle's garage and the same men Crane had met at the restaurant unloaded a dozen cartons. They contained everything Crane needed.

He started small. The first batch of stuff he cooked up could have been made by any reasonably competent chemist with access to some basic tools, the kind of junk that was sold out of trailers and skid row bars. But neither Crane's new business associates nor their customers had any complaints. Those associates suggested that he might want to expand his efforts and he told them, yes, he'd be glad to, but he needed a decent place to work. He couldn't produce quantity, much less quality, working in a toolshed. He told them what he had in mind and they told him it was no problem. Crane provided another shopping list and, three weeks after he had fled from the asylum, Crane moved into a large loft located in an industrial park on Gotham City's eastern border. Now, he had all that he needed, and it was time to begin his life's work again.

SEVEN

There were few people around the Major Crimes Unit headquarters tonight. Most of the on-duty crew were at the site of the afternoon's bank heist, and the rest were scattered throughout the boroughs investigating the odd homicide, a kidnapping or two, a few serious robberies. Only two cops were here, in the main bullpen: a twenty-year vet named Wuertz and relative newcomer Anna Ramirez.

Detective Ramirez was the duty officer, charged with taking calls and directing them to wherever they should go. She checked herself in a full-length mirror: She nodded, satisfied, and switched on the office television. She turned to the all-news channel and sat down in a chair near a bank of telephones.

Mike Engel, a local hotshot reporter, was on the screen, giving the mayor hell.

"Mister Mayor," Engel was saying, "you were elected on a campaign to clean up the city . . . When are you going to start?"

The mayor rubbed his lapel between a thumb and forefinger and said, "Well, Mike—"

Engel ignored him. "Like this so-called Batman—a lot of people say he's doing some good, that criminals are running scared. But I say he's not! What kind of hero needs to wear a mask? You don't let vigilantes run around *breaking the law*! Where does it end? Yet we hear rumors that instead of trying to arrest him, the cops are using him to do their dirty work."

"I'm told our men in the Major Crimes Unit are close to an arrest . . ."

Ramirez turned her eyes from the television and called to Wuertz, who was squinting at a sheet of yellow paper. "Hey, the mayor says you're closing in on the Batman."

Wuertz looked at her in distaste. "The investigation is ongoing."

He crumpled the yellow paper and tossed it at a corkboard on the nearest wall. The corkboard bore a strip of cardboard on which was lettered: BATMAN SUSPECTS. Below it were several pictures: Abraham Lincoln, Elvis, and the Abominable Snowman.

"Sure it is," Ramirez said, getting up and crossing to where a coffeepot perched atop a burner. She poured coffee into a plastic cup and went to a flight of stairs that led to the roof.

She found Lieutenant Gordon standing beside the newly installed searchlight that stabbed a beam of brightness into the sky above them. On misty nights, a bat silhouette on the searchlight's lens could be projected onto clouds, but, misty or not, the beam was always visible from anywhere in the city.

Ramirez handed the coffee to Gordon and asked, "Ever intend to see your wife again, Lieutenant?"

Gordon grunted and sipped the coffee. "How's your mother?"

"They checked her back into the hospital."

"I'm sorry."

"Least there she's got someone round the clock. Unlike your wife." Ramirez pointed her chin at the searchlight. "He hasn't shown?"

"No. But I like reminding everyone he's out there."

"Why wouldn't he come? You think he doesn't know this thing is for him?"

"Oh, he figured that out in a second. No . . . hopefully, he isn't here because he's busy."

EIGHT

Bruce Wayne wasn't the only person in Greater Gotham dressing up as the Batman that night—wasn't even one of two or three.

Brian Douglas still had his gym clothes on and was just about to have a shower and hit the sheets when he got the call from that weird guy, Anton-something, the guy who had organized the . . . Brian wasn't sure what it was. He thought of it as the "Batman Club." Two or three guys who stayed in touch and met occasionally for some vigilante action. Lonely guys, and angry guys—angry for good reason: all of them had suffered, in one way or another, from Gotham City's lawlessness. Douglas himself was an ex-cop who had gotten tired of the corruption and inaction in the police force and had decided to take matters into his own hands. According to this Anton, he had a second cousin who worked in a parking garage near the manufacturing district and he, the second cousin, happened to overhear two guys talking. The one with the thick Russian accent—at least Jimmy's cousin *thought* it was Russian and was sure it wasn't Spanish— told the other about a drug deal that was going down that night, in about an hour, in fact.

He hung up the phone and hauled his makeshift Batman suit out of the closet and put it on, then figured it wouldn't be too smart to wear a mask on the streets of Gotham this late at night. The mask with the pointy ears went into a coat pocket, then he reached for his shotgun. Checking it was loaded, he tucked it into his bulky coat and headed outside.

He got on his motorcycle, a Japanese model twenty-five years out of the showroom, and on the fifth try got the engine to kick over. Somebody from a window yelled at him to shut the damn thing off, but that was Gotham for you, people always complaining about something.

As he neared the parking garage Anton had told him about on the phone, he could see the two others in Bat-suits walking purposefully toward their common destination. He parked his bike on the sidewalk—at this hour, nobody would care—and joined his fellow Batmen.

The Chechen and his bodyguards got into his black SUV. While one of the men drove through the busy center of the city and into the industrial section, the Chechen and his other employees chatted. Someone mentioned the Batman, and the Chechen snorted.

"Fairy tales for little girls!"

———

Batman gazed through a tinted windshield and waited.

His Tumbler was parked on the roof across a narrow alleyway from a multifloored parking garage. During daylight hours, it would be jammed with cars and pickup trucks belonging to workers at the nearby storage facilities, but now, after dark, it was empty, as were the streets surrounding it. The Chechen and an unknown supplier of the drugs the Chechen peddled were to meet on the garage roof to do business. The Chechen went to considerable trouble to conceal his itinerary, and for a month he had succeeded. But eventually, patience, persistence, and no small amount of money had given Batman the knowledge he sought. It had taken him here.

He saw movement on the garage rooftop.

Two black SUVs were turning off the up ramp. They stopped near the only other vehicle on the floor, a battered white van. Several men, all of them bulky, all of them dressed in ill-fitting suits, emerged from the SUVs. The bulkiest of them looked out over the rooftops and suggested that there might be a night watchman on the premises.

The Chechen shrugged, and said in Russian, "That's why we bring the dogs."

He opened the back door of the nearest SUV, and

three enormous rottweilers sprang out, their claws clicking on the concrete floor. The Chechen knelt, and the dogs licked his face. He spoke again in Russian: "My little princes . . ." He looked up at the others. "The Batman's invisible to you fools, but my little princes . . . they can find human meat in complete darkness."

He left the dogs and went to the second SUV. He opened the back door and dragged out a filthy man wearing rags.

"No!" he squealed. "No, get 'em off me! Off me!"

The Chechen dragged his prisoner to the white van. The van's side door slid open, and two newcomers dressed in coveralls emerged, carrying metal kegs, guns strapped to their backs.

In heavily accented English, the Chechen said, "Look! Look what your drugs did to my customers."

From inside the van: "Buyer beware."

A tall, thin figure wearing a wrinkled blue suit and a burlap mask emerged from the van. "I told your man my compound would take you places. I never said they'd be places you *wanted* to go . . ."

"My business is *repeat* customers," the Chechen said.

"If you don't like what I have to offer, buy from someone else," the Scarecrow said. "Assuming Batman left anyone else to buy from."

Both of the dogs began barking in unison.

The barking grew louder.

"Come on out sonofbitch, whoever you are," the Chechen shouted, gazing around. "My dogs are hungry."

Suddenly a rising Batman silhouette appeared from around the corner. There was the roar of a shotgun and a ragged, round hole appeared in the SUV, inches from the Chechen.

More guns roared.

"Loose the dogs!" the Chechen screamed.

When nobody immediately obeyed him, the Chechen knelt by the rottweilers and snapped the leashes free from their collars. The dogs raced into the darkness. From an alcove leading to an elevator, a figure wearing a mask and cape stumbled toward the down ramp. One of the dogs leapt at him and closed its teeth and jaws on the Batman's neck.

The Scarecrow climbed into the driver's seat of the pellet-pocked van and stopped; the barrel of a shotgun was pressing into the back of his head. A mask with pointed ears was visible in the rearview mirror. The Scarecrow groped between the seats and lifted an aerosol can. He fingered a button, and a cloud of spray filled the van. The masked man dropped his shotgun and rolled, screaming, out the door. He lay crying at the Chechen's feet.

The Scarecrow stuck his head out, and said to the Chechen, "Not the real Batman."

"How you know?"

"We're old friends, the Batman and I."

"The other one ain't real either, I bet," a bodyguard said.

The Chechen kicked the whimpering man on the floor and was drawing back his foot to kick again when he stopped, startled by a loud crashing sound as four large wheels smashed down onto the concrete in front of him, dust and floor spraying everywhere.

"That's more like it!" said the Scarecrow.

Batman knew he had to be quick and effective and try not to hurt anyone too severely, especially not the fools in the costumes, whoever they were.

One of those fools stood nearby, lining up his shotgun on a fleeing bodyguard. Batman grabbed the weapon barrel and bent it upward as the faux Batman looked into the face of the red deal. He stumbled backward as Batman opened his hand to reveal a pneumatic mangle hidden in his palm.

He bore down on a pair of rottweilers mauling another costumed fool. Batman lifted his arm and drew a grappling gun. A monofilament shot out and wrapped around the fake Batman's ankle, and Batman pulled him away from the dogs.

Now the animals.

A rottweiler was already in the air, leaping at Batman's throat. Batman kicked it in the belly, and the dog fell away, whimpering. The second dog closed its jaws on Batman's gauntlet, but the Kevlar armor proved impenetrable. Batman swung the animal over his head and it fell to the concrete, whimpering.

While Batman had been busy with the rottweilers and the imposter Batmen, he saw Scarecrow climb into a van. He jumped aside as the van sped toward him. Then, as it passed, he put his fist through the driver's window. His armored knuckles grazed the Scarecrow's mask. Startled, the Scarecrow leaned away, unintentionally twisting the wheel. He righted it just in time to avoid smashing into a retaining wall, and the van skidded onto the exit ramp and began to descend it.

Batman sprang to the edge of the ramp and waited, staring down at the corkscrew-shaped ramp. If he went after the Scarecrow, the others might have time to run. If he didn't, the Scarecrow would certainly lose himself in the dark streets. *Six of one, half a dozen of the other* . . . But the Scarecrow was the known evil. Batman made his decision.

He jumped.

A second before he would have struck the ground, his cape expanded into glider wings that slowed his fall. The Scarecrow's van swerved out of the exit ramp, and Batman landed atop it, crushing the cab. The van swerved and struck a wall.

Batman pulled a dazed Scarecrow from the cab and slung him over his shoulder.

A minute later, he dumped the Scarecrow next to the Chechen's injured accomplices and two of the men wearing faux Batman costumes. The Chechen himself had disappeared.

"We're trying to help you," the impostor blurted.

"I don't need help," Batman said as he bound the Chechen's crew with plastic ties.

"Not my diagnosis," the Scarecrow said.

Batman stared at the Scarecrow as he fitted plastic ties over his wrists and ankles, then pulled off Crane's mask. Next he turned to the impostor. "Don't ever let me find you out here again."

"You need us! There's only one of you. It's war out here."

Batman walked toward his car carrying an armload of confiscated weapons and dropped them in a pile for the police.

"What gives you the right?" the impostor cried. "What's the difference between you and me?"

Batman replied, "I'm not wearing hockey pads."

The impostor looked down at his ridiculous outfit as Batman sped from the area.

At the last minute, Brian Douglas had decided not to join the other two Batmen in the parking garage. After all, he wasn't one of them, he was just an observer, and if he heard any kind of ruckus inside, maybe then he'd check it out. But otherwise . . . why hang around with a bunch of jerks? So Brian planted himself against a wall and waited. When he heard gunshots, he still waited.

Maybe somebody will come this way and I can ask them. There's no point in getting my ass shot off . . . That would be foolish . . .

That was why Brian saw Batman capture the Scarecrow, saw a distinctive silhouette swoop down to land atop the van and, without hesitation, without pausing for a second, reach into the damaged vehicle, haul the Scarecrow out, fling the criminal over his shoulder, and stride back into the garage. How long had the whole thing taken? Seconds—

—and then and there, Brian Douglas had an epiphany. Suddenly, he believed. He had seen something— some*one*—he had doubted. He was real, and he was magnificent, and Brian needed to know *more*!

The Chechen was furious, as angry with himself as with anyone else for allowing himself to become mixed up with such fools as the Scarecrow. Where were mobsters, thugs, greedy killers—the kind of criminal he understood, the kind of criminal he was himself? But he could not linger for revenge now. Everything had gone sour, and there was nothing for a sane man to do but escape. The Chechen had gotten behind the wheel of his SUV and roared away.

The cops waited until they were back at the station house before cutting the plastic ties from Jonathan Crane's wrists and confiscating his burlap mask.

"Well, well," a cop said, waving the mask. "We got us a celebrity."

"I think I liked him better with his face covered," another cop said.

NINE

Jim Gordon, in his unmarked squad car, heard someone he knew was Batman use police frequencies to call for patrol cars and ambulances. So it'd been right, what he'd told Ramirez—Batman *had* been busy. Good. But Gordon had other things on his mind, namely the bank heist that had happened earlier that day. He'd hoped to get Batman's insights into the crime; that's why he'd wasted an hour standing next to the searchlight. But Batman hadn't shown, and that shouldn't get in the way of Gordon doing his job, so it wouldn't.

He parked near a row of patrol cars. Ignoring shouts from reporters and gawkers, he entered the bank lobby.

For a while, he watched the forensics crew do its job. Then he called to a detective named McFarland, and asked, "We get anything from the surveillance cameras?"

McFarland handed Gordon a sheaf of grainy photographs. "He can't resist showing us his face."

Gordon looked at the pictures: a leering clown with a scarred mouth. Then he raised his eyes and glimpsed movement in the shadows near the tellers' cage.

"Be back in a minute," he told McFarland, and moved away.

He joined Batman in the darkness. "You made it."

Batman nodded and peered at the photos. "Him again. Who are the others?"

"Another bunch of small timers."

Batman said, "Get me some of the money."

Gordon went to where some twenty-dollar bills lay scattered on the floor next to Grumpy's body, scooped up a handful, and brought them to Batman, who scanned them with a gadget he'd taken from his belt. The gadget *ping*ed.

"Some of the marked bills I gave you," Batman said.

"My detectives have been making drug buys with them for weeks," Gordon said. "This bank was another drop for the mob. That makes five banks—we've found the bulk of their dirty cash."

"Time to move in."

Gordon waved a photo. "What about this Joker guy?"

"One man or the entire mob? The Joker will have to wait."

"We'll have to hit all the banks simultaneously— SWAT teams, backup . . ." Gordon held up a handful of banknotes. "When the new DA gets wind of this, he'll want in."

"Do you trust him?"

"Be hard to keep him out," Gordon said. "I hear he's as stubborn as you."

That last sentence was spoken to empty air. Gordon shrugged, then went to rejoin his detectives.

Alfred Pennyworth, whistling an old music hall ditty, moved through the Wayne penthouse, opening blinds, raising shades, stopping occasionally to admire the truly spectacular view from any of the windows. He went into the kitchen, placed a bowl of oatmeal and a cup of coffee on a tray and carried it to the bedroom. He stopped in the open room and frowned at the still-made bed.

Then he returned to the kitchen, filled a silver thermos with coffee, and took the elevator down to the building's garage.

Seven minutes later, he parked the Wayne limo in a corner of a railroad yard, got out, carried the thermos to a rusty freight container that sat, lopsided, on concrete blocks. He got a key from his vest pocket and opened a padlock on the container's hatch, then stepped inside.

A hiss. The floor lowered, taking Alfred down to the long, low-ceilinged concrete chamber he usually entered through a tunnel that led to Wayne's apartment building. But today, he thought it wise to assure himself that the elevator entrance was in working order, and was pleased to learn that it was. A hundred years ago, Hiram Wayne had this room built because he wanted to experiment with a steam-driven subway train. The train proved to be a bad idea, but the Wayne family had retained ownership of the ground Hiram had used for his experiments. This chamber had been forgotten by everyone, and although Bruce had heard it mentioned by an uncle, he doubted its existence until recent excavation had uncovered part of it. Bruce sensed that it might some day be useful and, again with the invaluable help of Alfred and Lucius Fox, had pumped out water, reinforced walls, done everything necessary to make it habitable.

Batman's massive vehicle sat in the center of the room, near a cluster of computers, printers, workbenches, power tools, and microwaves. Bruce sat amid the clutter, watching a television tuned to GCTV, the local all-news station.

"It will be nice when Wayne Manor is rebuilt, and you can swap not sleeping in a penthouse for not sleeping in a mansion," Alfred said, pouring coffee into the thermos cap.

Alfred handed the cap to Bruce and sat in a nearby chair to join his master. When the news report ended, Bruce returned to what he had obviously been doing when the broadcast had come on, stitching a gash on his arm from where one of the Chechen's dogs had bitten him.

Alfred took the needle from him, and said, "When you stitch yourself up you make a bloody mess."

"But I learn about my mistakes."

"You ought to be pretty knowledgeable by now, then." Alfred busied himself with doctoring.

"The problem this time was my armor," Bruce said. "I'm carrying too much weight. I need to be faster."

"I'm sure Mr. Fox can oblige." Alfred peered more closely at the wound. "Did you get mauled by a tiger?"

"A dog. A *big* dog."

For a while, neither man spoke. Finally, Bruce said, "There were more copycats last night, Alfred. With guns."

"Perhaps you could hire some of them and take weekends off."

"This wasn't exactly what I had in mind when I said I wanted to inspire people. I would never resort to guns or to killing *anyone*. These gang members are making it dangerous, Alfred. Innocents could be killed by their antics, and *I* don't want to shoulder the blame!"

"I know, Master Bruce. But things *are* improving. Look at the new district attorney."

"I am. Closely. I need to know if he can be trusted."

"Are you interested in his character . . . or his social circle?"

"Who Rachel spends her time with is her business."

"Well, I trust you're not following *me* on my day off." Alfred held up a stack of surveillance photos he saw on a side table. They were of Rachel Dawes with Harvey Dent, and they had obviously been taken over the past several weeks, perhaps even months. "Are you sure about that?"

"If you ever took one, I might," replied Bruce.

"Know your limits, Master Bruce."

"Batman has no limits."

"Well, *you* do."

"I can't afford to know them."

"And what happens the day you find out?"

"We all know how much you like to say, 'I told you so.'"

"*That* day, Master Bruce, even I won't want to. Probably."

TEN

The weather that Monday morning in Gotham City was gorgeous. It seemed that winter had finally gone, and spring had arrived. At 9:30, District Attorney Harvey Dent was running up the steps to the courthouse and at 9:31 he burst into one of the chambers. The courtroom was filled with lawyers, spectators, uniformed policemen, and Salvatore Maroni, who was to be tried that day.

"Sorry I'm late," Dent said to no one in particular as he sat at the prosecutor's table next to Rachel Dawes.

"Where were you?" Rachel whispered.

"Worried you'd have to step up?" Dent grinned and opened his attaché case.

"I know the briefs backward."

Dent's grin widened and he pulled a silver dollar from a pocket. "Well then, fair's fair. Heads, I'll take it. Tails, he's all yours."

Dent flipped the coin in the air, caught it, slapped it on his wrist, then uncovered it and displayed it to Rachel.

"Heads," Dent said. "You lose."

"You're flipping coins to see who leads?"

"My father's lucky coin. As I recall, it got me my first date with you."

"I'm serious, Harvey. You don't leave things like this to chance."

"I don't." Dent winked. "I make my own luck."

From the defendant's table across the aisle, Maroni said, "I thought the DA just played golf with the mayor, things like that."

"Tee off's one thirty. More than enough time to put you away for life, Sally."

The bailiff told everyone to rise, and court was in session. The judge entered and took his place at the bench, banged his gavel, and told Dent to call his first witness.

"I call Wilmer Rossi," Dent said.

Two uniformed guards brought in a thin man wearing a shabby suit. This was Wilmer Rossi. He sat in the witness box, was sworn in, and gazed at the approaching district attorney.

Dent leaned toward Rossi. "With Carmine Falcone in prison, someone must've stepped up to run the so-called 'family,' right?"

Rossi nodded.

"Is this man in the courtroom today?"

Again, Rossi nodded.

Dent turned his head to stare at Maroni. He was smiling. "Could you identify him for us, please?"

"You got me, Counselor," Rossi said. "It was me."

Dent turned back to Rossi, no longer smiling. "I've got a sworn statement from you that this man, Salvatore Maroni, is the new head of the Falcone crime family."

"Maroni? He's the fall guy. *I'm* the brains of the organization."

There was a brief burst of laughter from the gallery.

Dent looked up at the judge. "Permission to treat this witness as hostile."

"Hostile!" Rossi screamed. "I'll show you hostile!"

Rossi lifted his hand from his side, and somehow it was holding a gun. He aimed at Dent's face, barely four feet away, and pulled the trigger. There was a *click* as the gun's hammer fell on the firing pin, but there was no shot. Dent took a single step forward, grabbing the gun with his left hand as his right, curled into a fist, struck Rossi in the mouth. Rossi slumped back into the witness chair and spat blood.

Dent ejected the clip from Rossi's weapon, letting it fall to the floor, and crossed to where Maroni sat. He dropped the empty gun onto the table in front of Maroni, and said, casually, "Ceramic .28 caliber. That's how it beat the metal detectors. Made in China, I believe." Turning back to the witness box, he said, "Mr. Rossi, I recommend you buy American."

Dent straightened his tie and watched the bailiffs wrestle Rossi from the witness box.

"Your Honor," Dent said to the judge. "I'm not done with this witness. . . ."

An hour later, Dent was striding through the courthouse lobby with Rachel, who was panting slightly as she struggled to keep up with him.

"We'll never link that gun to Maroni," she said. "But I'll tell you one thing—the fact that they tried to kill you means we're getting to them."

"Glad you're so pleased, Rachel," Dent said. "Oh, by the way, I'm fine."

Rachel tugged at Dent's sleeve until he stopped. She smoothed his lapels. "Harvey, you're Gotham's DA. If you're not getting shot at, you're not doing your job. 'Course, if you said you were shaken, we could take the rest of the day off . . ."

"Can't. I dragged the head of the Major Crimes Unit down here."

"Jim Gordon? He's a friend. Try to be nice."

Dent and Rachel kissed good-bye, and he resumed walking. Dent turned down a short corridor and entered his office. James Gordon was already there. He stood and shook hands with Dent.

"Word is, you've got a hell of a right cross," Gordon said. "Shame Sal's going to walk."

"Well, good thing about the mob is they keep giving you a second chance."

Dent went to his desk and took a sheaf of currency from a drawer.

"Lightly irradiated bills," Gordon said.

"Fancy stuff for a city cop," Dent said. "Have help?"

"We liaise with various agencies—"

"Save it, Gordon. I want to meet *him*."

"Official policy is to arrest the vigilante known as the Batman on sight."

"And that floodlight atop headquarters?"

"If you have any concerns about . . . *malfunctioning equipment* . . . take them up with maintenance, Counselor."

Dent tossed the bills onto his desk, his annoyance visible. "I've put every known money launderer in Gotham behind bars. But the mob is still getting its money out. I think you and your 'friend' have found the last game in town, and you're trying to hit 'em where it hurts—their wallets. Bold. You gonna count me in?"

"In this town, the fewer people know something, the safer the operation."

"Gordon, I don't like that you've got your own *special* unit, and I don't like that it's full of cops I investigated at Internal Affairs."

"If I didn't work with cops you'd *investigated* while you were making your name in IA, I'd be working alone.

I don't get political points for being an idealist. I have to do the best I can with what I have."

"Look, Gordon, you want me to back warrants for search and seizure on five banks without telling me who we're after?"

"I can give you the names of the banks."

"Well, that's a start. I'll get you the warrants. But I want your trust."

"You don't have to sell me, Dent. We all know you're Gotham's white knight."

Dent grinned. "I hear they've got a different name for me down at MCU."

A mile uptown, Lucius Fox was presiding over a board meeting of Wayne Enterprises. Despite his impeccable suit and trim haircut, Fox did not much resemble what he, in fact, was—the CEO of Wayne Enterprises. There was nothing of the fat cat in his manner or appearance. Rather, he seemed to be what he *really* was, an inventor who also happened to have an IQ that was off the charts. Until his boss, Bruce Wayne, had returned from wherever it was he'd gone for seven years, Lucius was quite comfortable being a nonentity. He was known to be a favorite of Thomas Wayne, Bruce's father, and so the new cadre of executives who gradually took control of the company after Wayne's death didn't trust Lucius any more than he trusted them. They didn't fire him outright: He neither knew or cared why. Instead, they had exiled him to a department that did less and less business with every passing quarter, a department devoted more to research than quick-profit deals. Then they relocated that department to a subbasement, slashed its budget, put Lucius in charge of a staff they immediately discharged, and wished him the best of luck in his new endeavors. Fine with Lucius. More than fine. It felt like Christmas morning under the tree. He had all these toys to play with—others called them "research projects"—and plenty of time to play with them, all alone in his basement den. He kept his own hours, his own books, his own counsel.

As for money: The new occupant of the big office, William Earle by name, thought he was plenty smart, detail-oriented, the kind of captain who ran a tight ship. Fox thought he was a moron. Lucius had educated himself about computers before digital knowledge was a required subject for anyone with any desire to make a mark in American business because, to him, it was plain that computers would soon be essential tools, as necessary as cash registers had been in his father's time.

Bruce Wayne was Lucius Fox's candidate for the only man in Gotham City who might possibly be stupider than Earle. Then, unexpectedly, the young Wayne inserted himself into Fox's life. He was genuinely interested in what Fox was doing, and bright enough to comprehend it immediately. But Fox sensed that Bruce was more than merely curious. He wanted something. Make that plural—some*things*. Things like high-powered vehicles and body armor and climbing gear and weapons—not exactly the playthings of a wastrel.

Bruce never explained himself to Fox, but it was apparent that he did not doubt Fox's understanding of exactly what Bruce was doing with his nights. The pretense that Fox was blissfully unaware of the Bruce-Batman connection became a running joke between them.

Bruce changed Fox's life, utterly. After he and Bruce had collaborated on Earle's exit, Fox became the head of Wayne Enterprises, and was exhilarated to finally use his skills and intelligence to implement Thomas Wayne's vision. Fox privately described the empire he controlled as the "anti-Enron" of the East Coast. Good as all that was, Bruce's real contribution to Fox's happiness was what happened between the two of them and was never acknowledged: Fox's complicity in Bruce's nocturnal activities. Oh, the idea of fighting crime in a Halloween costume seemed ridiculous to Fox until he saw how effective it was becoming. Then he began to revel in his *own* secret identity: Batman's toolmaker. He and Bruce and a few others, like that Gordon fellow and the district attorney, Dent, seemed to be saving the city. That was worth doing and besides, he was enjoying himself. He'd imagined that by this point in his life, he'd be a mellow old guy who spent a lot of free time in parks and watching sports, generally being bored and frustrated. Instead, he not only had a mission, he *liked* having a mission, liked the challenges and the ability to focus his energy, experience, talent and intelligence on a single and highly worthy persona: *Batman's inventor.* Yes, indeed.

At the moment, he was sitting relaxed at a conference table, leaning forward a bit, listening intently to a dignified Asian man, wearing a suit far pricier than Fox's own. This was a man Lucius Fox knew as Mr. Lau, the president of a business entity that called itself L.S.I. Holdings. Seven other men, members of Fox's staff, sat around the table, all of them tapping out notes on laptop computers. Bruce Wayne was sitting at the head of the table, in front of a large window.

Lau was speaking: "In China, L.S.I. Holdings stands for dynamic new growth. A joint Chinese venture with Wayne Enterprises would result in a powerhouse."

Fox replied in a measured voice. "Well, Mr. Lau, I speak for the rest of the board, and Mr. Wayne, in expressing our own excitement."

Lau looked at the head of the table. Bruce Wayne's head was bowed, his chin resting on his chest, apparently asleep.

Everyone got up and quietly left the room.

Fox escorted Lau to the elevator, and as the doors opened, Lau said, "It's okay, Mr. Fox. Everyone knows who really runs Wayne Enterprises.

"We'll be in touch as soon as our people have wrapped up the due diligence," Fox said.

Lau nodded and entered the elevator. Fox watched the doors close and turned to where a lawyer named Coleman Reese was waiting.

"Sir, I know Mr. Wayne's not interested in how his trust fund gets replenished," Reese said. "But frankly, it's embarrassing."

The two men began walking down the corridor.

"You worry about the diligence, Mr. Reese," Fox said. "I'll worry about Bruce Wayne."

"It's done. The numbers are solid."

"Do it again. Wouldn't want the trust fund to run out, would we?"

Fox reentered the boardroom, where Bruce Wayne was now standing, gazing out the window.

"Another long night?" Fox asked.

Wayne turned, nodded, then smiled.

"This joint venture was your idea, and the consultants love it," Fox said. "But I'm not convinced. L.S.I.'s grown 8 percent annually, like clockwork. They must have a revenue stream that's off the books. Maybe even illegal."

"Okay," Bruce said. "Cancel the deal."

"You already knew?"

"I needed a closer look at the books."

"Anything else you can trouble me for?"

"Well . . . I do need a new suit."

Fox scrutinized his boss. "Three buttons *is* a little nineties."

"I'm not talking about fashion, Mr. Fox, so much as function."

Wayne took some large sheets of blue paper from an attaché case and spread them on the table. For the next few minutes, Fox examined the diagrams on them. Then he said, "You want to be able to turn your head."

"It would sure make backing out of the driveway easier," Bruce said, smiling.

"I'll see what I can do. I trust you don't need the new gear tonight."

"No, Mr. Fox, tonight I have a date with a ballerina."

ELEVEN

The Ocelot was Gotham's newest dining sensation. It was possible to spend a middle-class worker's monthly salary on a meal for six, if one went a little heavy on the wine. The food *was* spectacular; a fusion of French, Thai and, incredibly, St. Louis barbecue. It should have been ghastly; instead, it was delicious. But it wasn't the cuisine that drew most of its clientele to the Ocelot; it was the chance to be seen, and to let the world know that money was no object.

Rachel Dawes and Harvey Dent allowed themselves to be seated at a table in the center of the cavernous room. As they waited for menus, Dent looked around and frowned.

"It took three weeks to get a reservation, and I had to tell them I worked for the government."

Rachel raised her eyebrows. "Really?"

"This city's health inspector's not afraid to pull strings."

Rachel smiled, and half stood to look over Dent's shoulder at Bruce Wayne, who was entering accompanied by a beautiful woman. Wayne shooed away the maître d' and strode to Dent's table.

"Rachel!" Bruce said. "Fancy that."

"Yes, Bruce. Fancy that."

Bruce nodded to the woman standing next to him. "Rachel, this is Natascha. Natascha, Rachel."

In a pronounced Russian accent, Natascha said, "Hello."

Dent looked up at Bruce. "The famous Bruce Wayne. Rachel's told me everything about you."

"I certainly hope not."

Rachel said, "Bruce, this is Harvey Dent."

"Let's put a couple of tables together," Bruce suggested.

"Will they let us do that?" Dent asked.

"They should! I own the place."

"For how long?" Rachel asked. "Let me guess, about three weeks?"

Bruce stared at his shoes. "How'd you know?"

Rachel turned her gaze to Natascha. "Aren't you . . ."

"Prima ballerina for the Moscow Ballet," Bruce proclaimed.

"Harvey's taking me next week," Rachel said.

"You're into ballet, Harvey?" Bruce asked.

"No," Rachel said. "He knows *I* am."

Bruce motioned to the maître d' and whispered in his ear. A minute later, two busboys carried an extra table from the kitchen area and placed it next to Dent's.

"Let me order for everyone," Bruce said.

It was almost eleven when the four of them ate their last bite of dessert. The Ocelot was empty except for the wait staff and a handful of late diners.

Natascha dabbed at her lips with a napkin and continued the conversation they'd been having. "No, no, come on. How could you want to raise children in a city like this?"

"*I* was raised here," Bruce said in mock outrage, "and I turned out okay."

"Is Wayne Manor in the city limits?" Dent asked.

"Sure. You know, as our new DA, you *might* want to figure out where your jurisdiction ends."

"I am talking about the kind of city that idolizes a masked vigilante," Natascha said, her voice rising.

"Gotham's proud of an ordinary man standing up for what's right," Dent said.

Natascha shook her head. "No. Gotham needs heroes like *you*—elected officials, not a man who thinks he is above the law."

"Exactly," Bruce said. "Who appointed the Batman?"

"*We* did," Dent said. "All of us who stood by and let scum take control of our city."

"But this is a *democracy*, Harvey," Natascha said.

Dent leaned forward, his elbows and forearms on the table. "When their enemies were at the gate, the Romans would suspend democracy and appoint one man to protect the city. It wasn't considered an honor. It was considered a public service."

Rachel said, "And the last man they asked to protect the Republic was named Caesar. He never gave up that power."

"Well, I guess you either die a hero or live long enough to see yourself become a villain," Dent said. "Look, whoever the Batman is, he doesn't want to spend the rest of his life doing this. How could he? Batman's looking for someone to take up his mantle."

Natascha looked directly into Dent's eyes, smiled, and purred, "Someone like *you*, Mr. Dent?"

"Maybe. If I'm up to it."

Natascha leaned over the table and covered the top half of Dent's face with her flattened hands. "What if Harvey Dent *is* the Caped Crusader?"

Dent took Natascha's wrists and gently drew her arms away from his face. "If I were sneaking out every night, someone would've noticed by now."

Rachel glanced quickly at Bruce.

"Well, you've sold me," Bruce said to Dent. "I'm gonna throw you a fund-raiser."

"That's nice of you, Bruce. But I'm not up for reelection for three years. That fund-raising stuff won't start for—"

"I don't think you understand. One fund-raiser with *my* pals, you'll never need another cent."

The next day, the *Gotham Times*'s headline was:

WHO IS HARVEY DENT?

The paper tried to answer the question in a six-column profile that filled the entire front page of the *Metro* section. It began with basic biographical stuff: Public-school education; middle-class parents, father a cop, mother a housewife; scholarship to Gotham University, with history and pre-law majors; law school at the state university; both parents dead while Harvey was still a teenager; clerk for a supreme court judge; appointment to the Gotham City Internal Affairs Division and . . . from there on, Harvey was a meteor. Then, he snared one of the big prizes; he had been promoted to district attorney following the death of the previous DA. He wasn't the most popular man who ever held the job—the cops and courthouse guys hung nasty nicknames on him—but he was the most effective. He was sometimes slow to prosecute, but when he did, he won. *Period*.

He dated. No commitments, nothing that could be called a relationship, but he had no trouble finding attractive young women to share an evening with. No surprise there—he was a man on his way up, and, who knows, the last stop might even be the White House.

And he was handsome, as handsome as any leading man, as handsome as Bruce Wayne, and though he wasn't much of a dancer and not awfully good at small talk, he was socially adept enough to get through any reasonable social situation.

Hobbies? Well, he ran around the reservoir daily, and three times a week he used a gym near his office, but those activities weren't exactly recreational. They were like his high-protein, low-fat diet—tools to maximize his effectiveness. So, the answer to the hobby question was *no*.

The *Times* article was accompanied by a four-column color photo of Harvey Dent's head and shoulders. Handsome? Oh, yes indeed.

Rachel, knowing that Harvey seldom had time for newspapers, gave him a copy of the *Times*, which he tucked into his briefcase but did not actually forget about. He was curious about the profile, but he didn't want anyone to *know* he was curious. So the folded paper remained nestled among briefs and warrants until Dent was alone in his apartment, a bit after midnight. He checked his voice mail, listened to a message from Rachel, and debated calling her back, then decided not to; Rachel was an early-to-bed, early-to-rise kind of woman. He shucked his clothes, got into bed, and only then removed the *Times* from his briefcase and read about himself.

It didn't take long: Dent had taught himself speed-reading in law school. He threw the paper aside.

There were no errors of fact. But they got it all wrong.

Take Dad, for instance, and for openers: Police officer, member of Gotham's finest, badge and gun and nightstick and pressed blue uniform. Check. That's what the world saw, that's what made young Harvey the envy of kids whose fathers did things like drive trucks or tend bars. But what the world *didn't* see—*that* was the reality. The raging drunk. The smasher of dishes and furniture. And that nightstick . . . how many times had Harvey seen it slammed onto his mother's shoulders or across her belly? And when the neighbors called 911, and the uniforms arrived and saw Harry Dent, their brother-in-blue, they apologized for bothering him and left, and the beatings began again. Once, Harvey was hiding in the stairwell outside the apartment, he heard cops talking about his mother, about how before she married Harry she'd been *one of them* and probably deserved everything Harry gave her. Harvey didn't know what *one of them* was, but he did know that it was not a good thing to be called.

Lucy was his mother's name . . . He remembered her combing his hair and telling him what a *handsome* young man he was and how *proud* she made him. Sometimes her eyes were black, and sometimes her mouth was scabbed, but she always dressed and combed him and told him how wonderful he was.

The teachers at school echoed his mother. He was a

good boy, and a good-*looking* boy to boot, and he got good grades as well. He didn't believe it—how could a good boy have a father like his?—but he realized that as long as others believed it, he might be able to find a better life for his mother and himself.

When he was ten, his father moved out. His only explanation was, *I can't stand the sight of either of ya*. His father took a rented room near the precinct where he worked, and once Harvey saw him on the street with a middle-aged woman who resembled his mother, but Harry never visited, never sent birthday or Christmas cards. His parents did not get a divorce; people of their age and backgrounds simply did not *do* that. But they never lived together again or, Harvey believed, even saw each other until the night they both died. How that happened, how his estranged parents were in the same room, and what exactly they did or said to each other, neither Harvey nor any of the investigators ever learned. Harvey was late getting home that night: a school day, followed by his job at a local drugstore until ten. So it was almost ten thirty when he opened the apartment door and saw them: his mother with a knotted sheet around her neck, eyes open, feet dangling, hanging from a ceiling light fixture, and his father, gun in hand, lying on the floor beneath her, the wood under his hair soaked with blood. Harvey knew, immediately, without touching them, that they were dead, and he knew what he had to do: call the police, answer questions. The bodies were eventually put in bags and removed, and then Harvey was alone, in a dark apartment, filled with an unidentifiable odor and the creaks and groans of an old building: alone because he had no one, no relatives, no friends who could be awakened at three in the morning.

He didn't even try to sleep. He just sat staring out the front window at an empty street lined with tenements and tried to understand. Why had they done it? No, *what* was done? Did Mother kill Father, then hang herself? Or was it the other way around—he killed her, then himself? But if so, why did he hang her instead of just shooting her? Why had they been together? None of it made sense, and for Harvey, that was the worst part, the not-making-sense.

The sun rose, and Harvey showered, changed clothes, walked to school. A kid he didn't know mumbled *sorry* as Harvey passed him in the hall, and two others nodded to him, so Harvey knew that news of his parents' death was out there. Concerned teachers sent him to the guidance counselor, a kindly older woman who tried to get through Harvey's distant look. She made him promise to see a counselor, then Harvey asked to be excused. He remained silent and by himself for the remainder of the school day.

After school, he went to his job at the pharmacy. His boss stopped him as he was tying on his apron and said it was too bad, what happened to the mister and missus, and Harvey agreed, "Yeah, too bad."

On Saturday, he went to the church his mother sometimes attended and spoke to the pastor. The pastor said, "The Lord's plan is mysterious, all right, but someday you'll know this was all for the best, you just have to have faith."

Harvey never returned.

He didn't attend the prom, or any dances, or any football or basketball games. But he did study, and he did get those scholarships, and somewhere in there he discovered the Law, and he knew he'd found his profession. No, not merely profession—his vocation! The law made sense. The law transformed the chaos of human existence into logic, fairness, rules that were reasonable and could be obeyed. The law offered stability and structure, not only for Harvey Dent the citizen, but for Harvey Dent the orphan.

It was about the time that the Law revealed itself to Harvey that he became aware of what many thought was his greatest asset: his looks. He was, by any criterion, an extraordinarily handsome man. He himself could see that every morning when he looked in his bathroom mirror. It was odd: he could *see* it, but he didn't *believe* it. Well, okay, he didn't have to believe in something to use it. His face became a tool, like his intelligence and memory, and he would show it to the world and reap whatever benefits the display conferred.

He rose rapidly, playing by the rules, but playing *hard*. Part of the game was being seen with women, having the occasional romance, and he did these things, too, but he never found a female who interested him until he was introduced to Rachel Dawes.

At first, Harvey Dent was nothing more than a name to Rachel. He was the new guy working in association with the Internal Affairs Division, and, she heard, a wiseass and a fast gun. Not her type. She did not actually meet him until he began working in the DA's office, and that first time was briefly in court, and she had to like his looks—he was an extraordinarily handsome man. Which was another strike against him, really. By then, Rachel had had enough experience in the dating game to know something about men; one of the things she'd learned was that beautiful men tended to be more self-involved and egotistical than beautiful women. Their idea of a good time was to lean back and be admired. Not Rachel's idea. Not at all. But that day in court . . . the attorney in her had to admire his easy command of case law and the assertive way he presented his case. If he was impressed with his appearance, he concealed it well. He seemed totally focused on the business at hand and, again, the Rachel-the-lawyer liked what she saw.

Later, in the hall outside the courtroom, she caught up with him, told him she was an observer from the DA, and if her office could help in any way.

"Actually, there are a couple of items we should discuss," Dent said. "Buy you a cup of coffee?"

Rachel glanced at her watch. Half past five. She was officially off duty. "Okay," she said. "But we go Dutch."

"We'll see," Dent replied.

They strolled through rush-hour crowds to a diner favored by the courthouse set, went inside, ordered, then waited in a booth for their food. Dent took out his wallet.

"I said we'd go Dutch," Rachel reminded him.

"Okay," Harvey said. "Let's let fate decide."

He took a coin from his pocket, flipped it in the air, and as it was falling said, "Heads, I pick up the bill. Tails, it's yours."

He caught the coin and showed it to Rachel: heads.

He gave the waitress a five.

After several more cups and a shared piece of pie, Rachel told him, "I'm not impressed by your looks. Just so you know."

"We have something in common then. I'm not impressed by them, either."

Later, she said, "I lied, you know."

"How so?"

"I *am* impressed by your looks."

In coming months, she often remembered that hour they sat in a booth by the window, drank coffee, and discussed Dent's case. She was seeing another aspect of him: earnest, determined, sharing her own rage.

"There's nothing worse than a dirty cop," he told her. "My job—prosecuting them—doesn't win me any popularity contests, but it's necessary, and I love it."

"Love it?" Rachel asked, raising her brows.

"Funny way to put it, huh? But yeah, 'love' is the word. Guess that makes me pretty weird."

They sat and sipped in silence, watching pedestrians scurry past the window. After Dent's declaration, there seemed to be nothing more to say, but Rachel didn't want the conversation to end. That was when Rachel told Dent she was impressed with his looks after all.

TWELVE

Bruce Wayne saw them together in Gotham Park, in one of the horse-drawn buggies tourists liked to rent. They were sitting close together, deep in conversation, oblivious to the coachman sitting just in front of them, or the families out for a day's recreation, or the tourists snapping pictures, or Bruce Wayne, in his Lamborghini with a tall, sunglassed blonde in the next seat.

A few hours later, Bruce became Batman, and Batman delivered a pair of holdup men to police headquarters and arrived back at the penthouse early—just a bit after one.

Alfred, wearing pajamas and a robe, greeted him, and asked, "No need for needlework tonight?"

"No, not a single drop of blood shed—mine or theirs. Alfred, what do you think of Harvey Dent?"

"Where did *that* come from, Master Bruce?"

"You know who I'm talking about?"

"The new fellow in the District Attorney's Office?"

"That's him."

"I can't say I have an opinion. As the great Will Rogers said, 'All I know is what I read in the papers.' What is *your* opinion of Mr. Dent, Master Bruce?"

"He's too good to be true. His bio reads like . . . I don't know—like something a press office made up."

"That worries you?"

"Yes, it does. He's in a position where he could do a lot of harm."

"Miss Dawes works with him, doesn't she? Perhaps she could offer insight."

"I don't want to bother Rachel with it. She's got enough on her mind. I'll look into it myself."

Bruce Wayne had acquired a lot of skills, including superior detective skills. Some he'd gotten during the years he had bounced from university to university, preparing himself for a mission he had not yet defined for himself, some from his years with Rā's al Ghūl. "It's always useful to know as much as possible about your enemy," Rā's had once told him. Now, Bruce put everything he had learned to the task of getting to know Harvey Dent. What he got from hacking into computers was next to useless, but not quite: he didn't care about Dent's university grades, or the apartments he'd rented, but Bruce was glad to see the financial stuff—glad, but disappointed. Dent's bank accounts and credit-card activity were impeccable. He had neither spent nor received a single dollar that couldn't be accounted for. His police record was not quite as impeccable, he'd actually had a speeding ticket and three parking violations, none of which he'd questioned, all of which he'd settled promptly.

"*Nobody* is this virtuous," Bruce told Alfred.

"Perhaps you might consider speaking for yourself, Master Bruce."

"Point taken. *You* are a saint."

"I wouldn't say that. But you can."

Next, Bruce investigated the deaths of Dent's parents. At first, he had great difficulty concentrating on this task, and he didn't know why. Finally, he realized that Dent's tragedy paralleled his own: the loss of both mother and father, simultaneously, to violence. There were differences, of course. Bruce had been a child when he watched a man with a gun shoot Thomas and Martha Wayne, scattering Martha's pearls into the gutter, and vanish into the night. Dent had been well into his teens . . .

Perhaps old enough to have committed the crimes himself? It was an avenue worth pursuing. But that was not easily done. Any case more than ten years old was more than cold, it was frigid, hard to solve with every advantage even a modern police system can offer. And Gotham's was *not* a modern police system. There had been recent improvements, largely financed by the Wayne Foundation and implemented by James Gordon, but only information from the last year was reliably in

the brand-new computer's database. Before that . . .
Bruce knew of a ramshackle warehouse in South
Gotham full of cardboard boxes, tens of thousands of
them, stuffed with documents and even physical evi-
dence relating to crimes committed as long as a half
century earlier. Should Bruce Wayne request a guided
tour? But why would fun-loving Bruce be interested in
such serious antiques? That would be completely out of
character for him and might start people wondering.
Bruce remembered the lessons of his criminal mentor.
He'd spent several years being taught by Ducard without
ever once suspecting that Ducard was, in fact, Rā's al
Ghūl. Lesson: If you're going to wear a mask, be sure it
fits well.

Okay, Bruce was out. That left Batman.

It was ridiculously easy to break into the storage facility. It was on an old street paved with crumbling brick and
virtually unlit. There was only one car, a twenty-year-old
Chevrolet, parked near the building and that, Batman
guessed, was the watchman's ride. One watchman? Not
necessarily. He could have given a ride to colleagues.
Maybe other watchmen came by public transportation?
Not likely. There were no buses that ran in this neighborhood after six, and taxi fare would be too costly.

Okay, one for sure, and maybe more.

Batman went around to the rear of the facility, found
a broken window and . . . why not? Why do this the
hard way? Batman entered through the window and began to prowl. He heard the tinny sound of a cheap tele-

vision set coming from somewhere near the front of the first floor—no doubt the watchman, doing whatever he had to do to get through eight hours of tedium.

After an hour, Batman gave up. There was no system, no order here, just a vast jumble of boxes containing, probably, millions of items. There was also a lot of water damage—the sky was visible through holes in the roof—and a lot of rodent activity.

Batman exited through the broken window, slid through the shadows as he'd been taught to do until he reached the Tumbler, parked a mile away in the shadows. He considered his next move as he knew he would find nothing useful about Harvey Dent in the public records. Was anyone involved in the death of Dent's parents still alive and able to be questioned? Maybe Gordon could help.

He could, and did. Bruce had called him at home the next day, using the rough growl that was Batman's voice, and asked about the old case. Gordon knew of a detective who had worked on the case, retired just a few years, living in a fishing shack in New York's Adirondack Mountains. A man by the name of Al Grooms. The question was, how to approach Al Grooms? As Bruce Wayne? No—again, questioning Grooms is not something rich kid Bruce would do. Batman, then? He didn't want to scare—or challenge—Grooms, so maybe Batman wasn't such a good idea, either. Okay, a third choice.

Bruce reached Grooms by telephone and made a date to meet him the following Saturday. So, early Friday morning, Bruce donned a red wig, added a red moustache, adopted an aggressive strut very different from the walk of either Wayne or Batman, and drove the Lamborghini to New York. He spent a night at a motel and met Al Grooms at a coffee shop the next morning.

Grooms was a burly man, gone a bit round, dressed in jeans and a plaid shirt. In his day, he must have been tough and frightening. Bruce introduced himself as Charles Malone, a freelance journalist doing an article on Harvey Dent. At first, Grooms seemed reluctant to talk. Then, suddenly, it was as though a dam burst and the words poured out of him. Yeah, he remembered the Dent case. They wanted to pin it on the kid, him and the other officers working the case, but the kid, Harvey, really *was* at that damn drugstore all night, and they couldn't get enough to hold him, even in those days, when justice in Gotham was pretty much touch-and-go, or maybe lucky'd be a better word. Now, Harvey's old man was a perfect son of a bitch, worst cop on the force, and there was no shortage of skels'd like to put him down, and maybe a couple of decent citizens, too, but the truth was, he done the old lady, then he done himself, and good riddance to the both of them.

None of which answered the question of why they had gotten together.

Bruce thanked Al Grooms, paid for his lunch, gave the counterman an extra twenty to pay for Al's dinner, then drove south. By evening, he was having tea with Alfred.

He told Alfred about the meeting of Charles Malone and Al Grooms.

"Have you decided that Mr. Dent is the paragon he seems to be?" Alfred asked.

"No. There has to be *something* wrong with him."

"Perhaps what's wrong with him is that he seems to have captured the affections of Miss Dawes."

"I won't dignify that with a reply. Anything happen here while I was away?"

Bruce exhausted every possibility in investigating Harvey Dent: interviews—usually as Charles Malone—with teachers, classmates, old girlfriends, recent girlfriends, fellow prosecutors, defense lawyers, even convicts. He checked Dent's school transcripts as far back as junior high. He checked bar association documents. Nothing. Harvey Dent wasn't a saint, but he was a person of enormous integrity, courage, and ability.

Then he concentrated on Dent himself. For weeks, although he didn't know it, Harvey Dent had an unseen guardian angel. Batman followed him to and from his office, as well as the various courtrooms Dent frequented. Bruce Wayne, pretending to be interested in a female defendant, watched Dent conduct a major trial, and disguised as Charles Malone, watched Dent conduct several minor trials. All successfully, all with the utmost reticence. Finally, on a rainy Friday evening, Bruce saw Dent meet Rachel in the lobby of her apartment building.

She kissed Dent quickly but deeply on the lips, and Bruce realized that they were on another date.

Then he had an epiphany: *I'm jealous!* Upset and angry and . . . *jealous.*

He was in no condition to conduct surveillance and . . . Harvey Dent didn't *need* surveilling. Harvey Dent was *exactly* what he seemed to be, and what that was was a thoroughly admirable human being and, just possibly, the savior of Gotham City.

"I give up," he told Alfred. "I was wrong. The guy *is* a paragon. A much better man than I."

"Care to elaborate, Master Bruce?"

"He and I were dealt the same rotten hand. Parents dead through violence. But I had advantages . . . I had you and Rachel and now Lucius. I had a huge house and every option in the world. My financial resources were virtually unlimited."

"May I remind you that not everyone who pretended to be your friend was."

"You mean Earle? Yeah, he was a bad one, and there were a few others. But suppose they'd succeeded in getting my family's companies away from me? Do you think I'd've found myself begging for quarters on street corners? No, I'd've still lived very comfortably. By now, I'd be married to Rachel, and we'd have three kids and be deliriously happy."

"You can't be certain of that."

"No, but believe me, I wish I could. Well, maybe not the three kids part, but the rest—yes! It could have happened. Now look at Dent . . . as I said, same bad deal. Dead parents just like mine. No, wrong—*not* just like mine because *I know what happened*! It was tragic and ugly and pointless, but something like that occurs every day in every big city on Earth. There's really nothing mysterious about it. But Harvey . . . he'll go to his grave without being able to answer the biggest question in his life. And that's not the worst of it. I dug into his parents' finances. Know how much his mother had in the bank when she died? A hundred and fourteen dollars. Even back then, that was a pittance. His father was flat broke. He had nothing more than the few dollars in his pocket. No bank accounts. Months behind on his rent. Harvey had no resources at all, yet look what he accomplished. High school, college, law school, all on his own. Between studying and jobs, he couldn't have gotten more than four hours' sleep a night for years. But he persevered, and he achieved everything he set out to do."

"And now he wants to clean up Gotham City."

"Not just clean it up, Alfred. Remake it. Create a real Camelot."

"Small wonder Ms. Dawes is attracted to him."

"Rachel is Dent's one failure. This thing between them . . . it isn't real."

"No?"

"I know Rachel. She's . . . biding time. Waiting for the right person."

"And that would be?"

Bruce shrugged.

THIRTEEN

Harvey Dent became the flavor of the week. The story in the *Times* was picked up by other papers, including some from other nearby states The three local magazines did pieces on Dent, which prompted the big television stations to pay attention. The Harvey Dent story was featured on all the cable news outlets and even merited a thirty-second spot on two of the networks' evening news shows. Every report mentioned the usual kinds of stuff, Dent's law-school career, his uprooting of corrupt cops and, of course, the biggie—his courtroom heroics after Rossi pulled his ceramic gun, caught by a spectator with a camera phone who made enough selling the image to pay for her daughter's Ivy League education. And they all showed pictures of the Dent visage; the racket-busting DA looked even better on television than he did in person.

One of the more prominent talking heads ended his nightly cablecast by staring into the camera, radiating his usual steely sincerity, and telling the nation: "We're sick of it, aren't we? You know what I'm talking about. The stink that's been coming from the corridors of power for years, from the domed havens of the panderers and pimps, from the courts, the cop houses, the capitals, and the Long Shore mansions. It reeks, and I want to puke, and I'm betting you do, too. The people of Gotham City—I know they want to puke, because plenty of them have told me so. They're so desperate, those Gothamites, that they adopted a hero. Did I say hero? What I mean is, *buffoon*. I mean, ask yourself, what kind of man dresses up in a funny suit and a mask? Yeah, you got it—a *buffoon*! But now, hey—take a look. Gotham's got itself a *new* hero, and this one's the genuine article. No cape and pointy ears on this guy. He wears a suit and tie, and he's plenty smart in the book sense of smart, but he can handle himself on his feet, too. A creep named Rossi learned that the hard way when he pulled a gun made of some sort of Silly Putty and got his clock cleaned by a sweet right cross. And who threw that kayoer? The man I've been talking about, Gotham City's *real* knight in shining armor, District Attorney Harry Dent. Fly away, batty boy, Dent's gonna get the job done."

The following night, the talking head apologized for calling Harvey "Harry," but the apology wasn't really necessary. Everyone who saw the show and could possibly care knew who he meant, and a lot of people agreed with him.

Alfred Pennyworth did not agree, but his boss did.

"I think the only buffoon involved here is the one making the noise," Alfred said.

"I think there's a lot in what he says," Bruce said.

Alfred waited for Bruce to elaborate, and when that didn't happen, excused himself to attend to household chores.

Harvey Dent didn't agree with the talking heads either. He didn't express his reservations publicly and, in fact, cooperated with the media's veneration of him. He didn't accept invitations to fly to New York, Chicago, Atlanta, or Los Angeles to be interviewed face-to-face, but he did allow a few camera crews into his office and apartment, and twice traveled to local studios for remote interviews being conducted by people hundreds of miles away.

Driving away from one of those, he confided to Rachel, who was at the wheel, "They're wrong about Batman . . . at least, I think they are."

"Want to tell my why?" Rachel asked.

"From my new vantage point, my new job, I can see the limitations of what I do. Rachel, the corruption in this town is so deep, so pervasive . . . it's in the air we breathe. And I can't beat it. There are places I can't go, things I can't do. I'm like a surgeon who's only allowed to cut skin deep. I'll never get to the cause of the problem."

"You believe in the law . . ."

"Yes! Yes, I do. But I've come to see that it has limitations. First, we need to rid ourselves of the corruption, because as long as we're corrupt, the law can't function. When the evil's gone . . . *then* the law takes over, restores order, creates the climate in which civilization can flourish. But not until the evil's gone."

"I've never heard you use the word 'evil' before."

"Dammit, that's what it is. I'm sick of euphemisms. Evil I said, and evil I meant, and we have to cleanse ourselves of it."

"How does Batman come into this?"

"As a partner, I hope. I said there's a limit to what I can do, operating on my side of the law. The same is true for him. We have to work together, Batman and I."

"You want him to be your shadow?"

"Exactly. A good way to put it—my shadow. He goes where I can't, he does what I shouldn't. Using what he gives me, I go into court and do what *he* can't. Together, we clean up Gotham."

"Suppose you do? What happens to Batman when you're finished?"

"Good question. I wish I had a good answer. I'd like to believe he'll survive, maybe just go away and never be seen or heard from again. But we all take our chances."

Rachel was silent for the rest of the drive.

The neighborhood around the Thomasina Arms had once been what the newspaper columnists of the day called "swanky." But that was years ago. Now, it had deteriorated to a welter of shabby rooming houses, cheap bars—a region of darkness, not least because every one of the streetlamps had been shattered, either by bullets or rocks. The Thomasina Arms—the "Tommy," as locals called it—had gone from being the home-away-from-home of visiting dignitaries to a single-occupancy hotel frequented mostly by dreary individuals who did not want to be seen any more than was necessary.

But it did have metal detectors, and some of the burly men lounging in the lobby had bulges under their jackets. The Chechen and another man moved through the detector under the impassive gazes of two Chinese with pistols shoved into their belts.

The Chechen turned to the man beside him. "You Gambol? From east side?"

"Yeah," Gambol replied. They went to a shadowy flight of stairs and trudged up to a kitchen on the second floor.

Inside, there was a small table, its surface scratched and discolored. Around it sat an ethnically mixed array of middle-aged men, most of them wearing expensive suits. Two Chinese, who could have been twins of the pair at the metal detector, brought in a television set, put it on the table, plugged it in.

"The hell is this?" Gambol demanded.

The television screen flickered, brightened, then everyone was staring at the face of Mr. Lau. Several of the men around the table rose from their chairs, muttering complaints.

"Gentlemen, please," Lau said, his voice pitched low, barely audible. The men who had risen resumed sitting, and Lau continued: "As you're all aware, one of our deposits was stolen. A relatively small amount—68 million."

"Who stupid enough to steal from us?" the Chechen yelled.

"I'm told the man who arranged the heist calls himself the Joker."

"What the hell is *that*?"

Sal Maroni, who had been sitting with a surly expression on his face, said, "Two-bit whack job wears a cheap suit and makeup. He's not the problem—he's a nobody. The *problem* is our money being tracked by the cops."

Lau said, "Thanks to Mr. Maroni's well-placed sources, we know that police have indeed identified our banks using marked bills and are planning to seize your funds today."

Everyone in the room began to shout.

The Chechen's voice was loudest: "You promise safe, clean money launder."

Lau waited for the noise to abate. Then he said, "With the investigation ongoing, none of you can risk hanging on to your own proceeds. And since the enthusiastic new DA has put all my competitors out of business, I am your only option."

"So what are you proposing?" Maroni asked.

"Moving all deposits to one secure location. Not a bank."

"Where, then?"

"Obviously, no one can know but me. If the police were to gain leverage over one of you, everyone's money would be at stake."

"What will stop them from getting to you?" the Chechen demanded.

"As the money is moved, I go to Hong Kong. Far from Dent's jurisdiction. And the Chinese will not extradite one of their own."

It started as a giggle and grew to a chuckle, then the Joker stepped from an adjoining room, his laughter becoming a shriek.

He stopped laughing, and said, "I thought *I* told the bad jokes."

"Give me one reason I shouldn't have my boy here"—Gambol indicated a bodyguard with a jerk of his thumb—"pull your head off."

The Joker took a freshly sharpened pencil from his hip pocket and placed it, eraser down, on the table. "How about a magic trick?" he asked brightly. "I'll make this pencil disappear."

Maroni's thug lunged. The Joker sidestepped, gripped the back of the thug's head, and slammed it down onto the pencil. The thug's body went limp and slid to the floor.

The pencil was gone.

"Magic," the Joker declared. "And by the way, the suit wasn't cheap. You should know. *You* bought it."

"Sit," the Chechen said to the Joker. "I wanna hear deal."

"A year ago, these cops and lawyers wouldn't dare cross any of you," the Joker said. "What happened? Did your balls drop off? See, a guy like me—"

"A freak," Maroni said.

The Joker ignored him and continued, "A guy like me . . . I know why you're holding your little group-therapy session in broad daylight. I know why you're afraid to go out at night. *Batman.* He's shown Gotham your true colors. And Dent's just the beginning." He pointed to the television set. "And as for his so-called plan—Batman *has* no jurisdiction. He'll find him and make him squeal." He smiled at Lau's image on the screen. "I can tell the squealers every time."

"What you think we should do?" the Chechen asked.

"It's simple. Kill the Batman."

"If it's so easy, why haven't you done it already?" Maroni growled.

"Like my mother used to tell me, if you're good at something, never do it for free."

"How much you want?" the Chechen asked.

"Half."

The men around the table laughed.

The Joker shrugged. "You don't deal with this now, soon Gambol won't be able to get a nickel for his grandma—"

Gambol bolted to his feet. "*Enough* of the clown."

He came around a corner of the table and stopped. The Joker had opened his coat, revealing explosives strapped to his chest.

"Let's not blow this out of proportion," the Joker said.

Gambol moved a step closer. "You think you can steal from us and just walk away? I'm putting the word out—five hundred grand for this clown dead. A million alive, so I get to teach him some manners first."

"Let me know when you change your minds," the Joker said, and strolled from the room.

"How soon can you move the money?" Maroni asked Lau.

"I already have. For obvious reasons, I couldn't wait for your permission. But rest assured, your money is safe."

Sal Maroni decided he didn't like some fruitcake he knew nothing about sticking his nose where it didn't belong. He knew this private eye, ex-cop, kicked off the force for taking bribes, not for lack of ability. Ability-wise, he was as good as they get. Name of Hamlin. Did some jobs for Sal now and then. Charged plenty, but always delivered. Sal called Hamlin and said, *I wanna know everything about this Joker down to his shoe size* and Hamlin said, *Gimme a couple weeks, I'll be in touch.* A couple of weeks passed and Hamlin called. *I ain't found anything yet, gimme a little more time.* Sal gave him a little more time. A week later, Hamlin showed up at the club in the middle of the afternoon, drinking coffee from a plastic cup and looking like hell. He needed a shave and a haircut. He had lost weight, and his suit was wrinkled and hanging off him, his tie had a big gravy stain on it, and there were dark bags under both eyes . . . *I dunno where to go next. Three weeks now, I been looking at this Joker and know what I see? Nothing. Driving me nuts. You sure he's real? You ain't imagining him, are you? 'Cause it's like he popped up outta thin air or something.* Sal didn't like what he was hearing, said, *You ain't messing with me, are you? I'm thinking maybe this Joker gets to you, slips you a little something to keep your mouth shut*, and Hamlin said, *You know that ain't me, Sal, hell, you and me, we go back*, then Hamlin started to laugh, and the laughing got louder and pretty soon it wasn't so much a laugh as it was Hamlin gasping for air. Hamlin was choking, his eyes were bulging, his face was crimson. Sal yelled to a waiter to get a glass of water, but by the time the waiter came with it, Hamlin was dead.

Sal had his own personal doctor do an autopsy, but he should have saved the money. It didn't take a medico to figure out that Hamlin was poisoned by the coffee he was drinking, anybody could've seen that, and as for the rest . . . Okay, the poison was some kind of stuff you can only get in China, Tibet, Korea, one of those places, and who cares?

Harvey Dent had been standing on the roof of police headquarters next to the searchlight, which was sending its beam into the sky for twenty minutes when he suddenly realized that he was not alone.

"You're a hard man to reach," he told Batman.

Then the door to the stairwell slammed open and Gordon, gun in hand, burst onto the roof. He looked at Dent and Batman, holstered his weapon and, ignoring Batman, approached Dent.

"You *don't* turn the signal on without my permission!" said Gordon.

"And you don't move on the mob without telling *me*," replied Dent. "Lau's halfway to Hong Kong," he continued. "If you'd asked, I could have taken his passport. I told you to keep me in the loop."

"Yeah? All that was left in the vault were the marked bills. They knew we were coming. As soon as your office gets involved, there's a leak."

"*My* office? You're sitting down here with scum like Wuertz and Ramirez . . . Oh yeah, Gordon, I almost had your rookie cold on a racketeering beef."

"Don't try to cloud the fact that Maroni's clearly got people in your office, Dent."

Dent turned to Batman. "We need Lau back, but the

Chinese won't extradite a national under any circumstances."

"If I get him to you," Batman asked, "can you get him to talk?"

"I'll get him to *sing*."

"We're going after the mob's life savings," Gordon said. "Things *will* get ugly."

"I knew the risks when I took the job, Lieutenant. Same as you." Dent turned. "How will you get him back?"

But Batman wasn't there.

"He does that," Gordon said.

The next morning, Lucius Fox found his boss waiting when he arrived at his office just before seven. Fox nodded to Bruce Wayne and sat behind his desk.

"Our Chinese friend left town before I could tell him that the deal's off," he said.

"I'm sure you've always wanted to go to Hong Kong," Bruce said.

"What's wrong with a phone call?"

"I think Mr. Lau deserves a more personal touch," Bruce said. "Now about my wardrobe problem . . ."

"Come with me."

They entered a private elevator and descended to a subbasement, which housed the company's Applied Sciences Division. On the way there, Bruce filled Lucius in on another task he had for him. Applied Sciences was an area Fox knew well; until recently, it had been his domain. He led Bruce to a space cluttered with workbenches, filing cabinets, and unopened cartons.

". . . high-altitude jumps," Fox was saying. "You need oxygen and stabilizers. I must say, compared to your usual requests, jumping out of a plane is pretty straightforward."

He stopped at a cabinet, pulled open a drawer, and hauled out an oxygen tank and ribbed rubber hosing.

"How about getting back into the plane?" Bruce asked.

"I recommend a good travel agent."

"Without the plane landing."

"That's more like it, Mr. Wayne."

Fox shut the drawer and rubbed his chin. "I don't think I have anything here. The CIA had a program in the sixties for getting their people out of hot spots called 'Sky Hook.' I'll work on it. For now—"

He pulled open another drawer. Inside were the components to a Batman costume. Bruce lifted a sleeve that bore scalloped blades.

"Hardened Kevlar plates on a titanium-dipped fiber triweave for flexibility," Fox said, pride in his voice. "You'll be faster, lighter, more agile."

As Bruce inspected the gauntlet, the blades suddenly shot from the sleeve and spun across the room to embed themselves in a wall.

Fox chuckled. "Perhaps you should read the instructions first."

"Sounds like a good idea."

Fox lifted the costume's chest piece and bent and twisted it, demonstrating its flexibility. "There *is* a trade-off, however . . . The spread of the plates gives you weak spots. You'll be more vulnerable to gunfire and knives."

"We wouldn't want things getting too easy, would we? How will it hold up against dogs?"

"You talking Chihuahuas or rottweilers? It should do fine against cats."

Later, driving out of the city in his Lamborghini, Bruce called Alfred.

"I found a Navy cargo plane in Arizona," Alfred said. "Very nice. The gentleman says it will take him a week to get it running. And he takes cash. What about a flight crew?"

"South Korean smugglers. They run flights into Pyongyang, below radar the whole way. Did you think of an alibi?"

"Oh, yes."

Rachel and Harvey's exciting night at the ballet became, instead, a quick cup of coffee at a café and an early return home. They had arrived at the theater to find it closed. Someone had taped the front page of a tabloid onto the box office window. There was a photograph of a smiling Bruce Wayne, wearing a short-sleeved white shirt and a beaked cap under the headline:

**LOVE BOAT—BILLIONAIRE ABSCONDS
WITH ENTIRE MOSCOW BALLET**

FOURTEEN

Bruce seemed to be enjoying himself. He stood on the deck of a ninety-foot yacht, watching the sunlight glittering on a calm sea, occasionally glancing over his shoulder at the dozen young women who wore swimming suits and were lounging around the deck on towels.

Alfred, standing next to Bruce, said, "The ladies seem to be quite healthy."

"Ballerinas have to stay in shape," Bruce said.

Both men looked upward, alerted by the buzz of an airplane, which was swooping in for a landing.

"I believe your transportation has arrived," Alfred said.

"So it would seem. You look tired, Alfred. Will you be all right without me?"

"If you can tell me the Russian for 'apply your own bloody suntan lotion.'"

Bruce stood and faced the sunbathing dancers. "Ladies," he shouted, "something's come up, and I must leave your charming company. I may or may not be back. In any case, Mr. Pennyworth is your host, and he'll see to it that you get anything you need. Have a nice day."

Bruce waved, kicked off his deck shoes, tossed a large, waterproof bag into the water, and jumped in after it. He snagged the bag and began to swim toward the plane.

Later, in the air, leaning against the plane's curved bulkhead, Bruce found himself thinking of Rachel. She'd see the media stuff about his sojourn with the ballerinas—in fact, if she didn't see it, he would have failed. And she would probably realize that it was some kind of ruse, but would she be at all jealous? And would she seek comfort with Harvey Dent? He did not want to think about the obvious answer to that . . .

The poolroom next to the Thomasina Arms was surprisingly deserted given its hip and trendy reputation. A sleek lamp, hanging from the ceiling was burning over a table as music thumped in the background. Gambol tried to sink the seven ball with a cushion shot, missed, and cursed. A burly man stepped into the light and told Gambol that someone had come to see him. Several someones, as a matter of fact.

"They say they've killed the Joker," the man continued. "They've come for the reward."

"They bring proof?" Gambol asked.

"They say they've brought the body."

Two newcomers entered the poolroom lugging what was obviously a body wrapped in plastic garbage bags. They dropped it at Gambol's feet and stepped away. Gambol's men crouched near the body and Gambol tore away one of the bags, revealing the scarred face of the Joker. Gambol spat at it and turned to the bounty hunters.

"Dead, you get five hundred—"

The Joker sat upright and threw knives into the chests of Gambol's two men.

"How about alive?" The Joker giggled.

Gambol turned and gasped. The Joker thrust an open switchblade into Gambol's mouth and pushed against a cheek.

"Wanna know how I got these scars?" the Joker asked, moving his face forward until it almost touched Gambol's. "My father was a drinker and a fiend. He'd beat mommy right in front of me. One night, he goes off crazier than usual, mommy gets the kitchen knife to defend herself. He doesn't like that. Not. One. Bit."

The Joker pivoted the blade to Gambol's other cheek.

"So, me watching, he takes the knife to her, laughing while he does it. Turns to me, and says, 'Why so serious?' Comes at me with the knife—'Why so serious?'

Sticks the blade in my mouth. 'Let's put a *smile* on that face' and . . ."

The Joker stared into Gambol's eyes. " 'Why so serious?' "

The Joker quickly moved the knife, and Gambol gurgled blood and fell to the floor.

Lucius Fox stepped from the helicopter, his hair ruffled by the still-whirling rotor. Two Chinese men dressed in business suits got out of a town car and trotted over to shake hands with Fox.

"Welcome to Hong Kong, Mr. Fox," the older man said. "Mr. Lau regrets he is unable to meet you in person, but with his current legal difficulties . . ."

"I understand," Fox said.

They all climbed into the town car and were soon gliding through the city, the men pointing out places of particular interest to Fox. The car stopped in front of a very modern building with two glass towers called IC1 and IC2. The men led Fox into the lobby to a desk where uniformed guards stood waiting.

"I'm afraid for security reasons I have to ask for your mobile phone," a guard said to Fox.

Fox nodded, smiled, and gave the guard his cell phone. Then Fox and his escorts went to a second-floor dining room, where they were met by Lau. Lau and Fox took seats at a table that looked out onto beautifully tended gardens, and ordered lunch from a waiter in a meticulous white jacket.

"I must apologize for leaving Gotham in the middle of our negotiations," Lau said. "The *misunderstanding* with the Gotham Police Force . . . I couldn't let such a thing threaten my company. A businessman of your stature will understand. But with you here . . . we can continue."

"It was good of you to bring me out here in such style, Mr. Lau," Fox said. "But I've actually come—"

Fox was interrupted by the tinkling sound from his side pocket. He pulled out a phone identical to the one he had given the guard.

Lau said, visibly irritated, "We do not allow telephones—"

"Sorry," Fox said. "Forgot I had it." He turned off the phone and placed it on the table in front of him. "Where were we . . . Oh, yes. I've come to explain why we're going to have to put our deal on *hold*. We can't afford to be seen doing business with . . . well, whatever it is you're accused of being. A businessman of your stature will understand."

Lau rose. Fox put his phone back in his jacket and stood up.

"I think, Mr. Fox, that a simple call might have sufficed," Lau said.

"Well, I do love Chinese food. And Mr. Wayne didn't want you to think we'd been deliberately wasting your time."

"Just accidentally wasting it."

Fox laughed. "That's very good. *Accidentally*. Very good. I'll be sure and tell Mr. Wayne that he was wrong about you not having a sense of humor."

Fox nodded pleasantly and went alone to the elevator. In the lobby, the guard tried to return his phone, but Fox shook his head no and pulled the identical working phone from his pocket. The guard frowned after him as Fox left the building.

Bruce Wayne stood on a public escalator aiming a camera at the skyline and behaving like a tourist. Lucius Fox joined him.

"There's a better view from the peak tram," Fox said.

"How's the view from L.S.I. Holdings?"

"Restricted. Lau's holed up there good and tight."

Fox held out his cell phone.

"What's this?" Bruce asked.

"I had R&D work it up. It sends out high-frequencies and records the response time to map an environment."

"Just like a ba—"

"Submarine," Fox said quickly. "Like a submarine."

"And the other device?"

"In place."

Bruce began sauntering away.

"Mr. Wayne?" Fox called. "Good luck."

Bruce spent the rest of the day behaving like a tourist and, to his surprise, actually enjoying himself. It wasn't his first visit to Hong Kong, but it was far more pleasant than his earlier sojourn here. That had been a lifetime ago, when Batman did not yet exist, except as the dimmest of notions, and Bruce was hopping from country to country, city to city, learning the ways of the world's criminals and occasionally—inevitably—participating in their activities. He had come late at night the hard way, by rowing a dinghy from a freighter anchored two miles offshore and tying the boat to a small pier sometimes used by fisherman. He was supposed to meet a Chinese national who would give him a package. He was to return the package to the freighter, and that would end the deal. But the man he was to meet never came. Bruce stayed near the pier until dawn. He rowed out to where the freighter had been and found the ship gone. He was alone in a strange country with no local currency, no identification, no resources. He was also shaggy. He had a long, greasy beard and hair that hadn't been cut in six months. His clothes were greasy from his work in the freighter's engine room, and he badly needed a bath. The next week was interesting, but he survived and eventually left Hong Kong by sneaking into the engine room of a luxury liner, where his appearance was actually an asset, and stowing away until the ship docked in Sydney, where he'd met a young American named Zachary Dabb, who was doing some kind of charity work with the Aborigines. Bruce left after a week, but Dabb was on his Christmas gift list, along with ten thousand other close friends. He sometimes wondered what Dabb did with the kind of gifts Wayne Enterprises mailed out.

The adventure had taught him a lesson. He'd gone into it knowing nothing about what was in the package, who was supposed to deliver it to him, what he should do in the event of a snafu. He had been stupid. The Boy Scouts had it half-right: *Be prepared.* Rā's al Ghūl supplied the other half: *But don't count on your preparations.*

Just after dark, he got his bag from the public locker where he'd stored it and went to Lau's office complex. There were two towers. One had less security than the other, a few guards patrolling the grounds and a handful of security cameras, all of which were ridiculously easy to avoid. The more secure tower was where Lau had his offices and computer stations, and that was bathed in light from lamps spotted every few feet along its foundations. Bruce could see motion detectors and a veritable army of guards, weapons on their belts and slung across their backs. All this confirmed what Fox had described. He climbed to the taller tower across from the shorter tower. Fox had visited earlier, the one with all the protection. There, he removed his Batman suit from his bag and put it on. From a distance, it would look like the costumes he wore in Gotham City, but instead of a cape, Batman had what looked like a hard plastic pack on his back. He removed two black boxes from his utility belt, and with a few clicks put them together to form a device that resembled a rifle. Batman lifted it to his shoulder, scoped the shorter tower, and squeezed the trigger four times. Four small sticky bombs shot from the barrel and adhered to windows of the top floor of the smaller tower. Each had visible timers that were counting down the seconds rapidly.

In the lobby below, the phone Fox had left behind began to glow. The top-floor lights dimmed and, suddenly, all the doors hissed open.

A guard looked around, then used his radio to call for help.

Batman launched himself into the empty air between the buildings. His backpack burst open and re-formed itself into wide, stiff glider wings. His descent slowed, and he streaked around the shorter tower, then banked hard to line up with a window in the rear.

He cannonballed into Lau's office, a hail of shattered glass surrounding him, and with the flick of his wrists, his wings again re-formed themselves, this time into a soft cape he wrapped around himself. He hit the floor, rolled, then stood upright and removed Fox's second phone from his belt. He took only a second to glance at the screen, on which was a diagram of the building he had just entered, then moved quietly into a corridor. He could hear shouts from below and the wail of approaching sirens.

Lau did not know what was happening, but he *did* know that whatever it was couldn't be good. He decided that caution was his best response and locked himself in his office. From a desk drawer, he took a fifty-caliber semi-automatic pistol and a flashlight. He switched on the light and swept it around the office. Nothing. Nobody here.

Then the door exploded inward and fell onto the rug, and something struck the flashlight from his hand, extinguishing it.

Lau fired in the direction of the door, then fired again.

Below, a dozen policemen, wearing helmets and holding assault rifles at port arms, swarmed into the building. One of Lau's guards pointed first to an elevator and then to the fire stairs. Half the cops ran to the elevator, the other half to the stairs.

Lau was on his feet, shooting into the blackness that surrounded him, the muzzle flashes from his weapon lighting the office for less than a second each. He fired his last round and in the brief red blaze saw a black silhouette, a giant bat, swooping toward him.

Batman had been mentally counting the seconds since he had burst into Lau's sanctum. He hit the man once, feeling a flush of satisfaction as Lau immediately fell. He removed a pack from under his cape, a smaller version of the one that had converted into wings, then the cape itself, and strapped it onto Lau.

Still counting seconds. *Ten, nine, eight* . . .

Almost time. . . .

five, four, three, two . . .

The four small, round sticky bombs Batman had launched onto the wall exploded simultaneously, rending steel, glass, and cement, opening a jagged gap to the dawn sky over Hong Kong, just as the six cops who had ridden the elevator up followed their flashlight beams and gun barrels into the room. The air was filled with thick dust from the explosions, making it impossible for the cops to see clearly. But they could hear a low rumble, coming closer . . .

Batman jerked a cord attached to the pack he'd fixed to Lau, and a weather balloon exploded out and began inflating, unreeling high-test nylon. The cops flashed their weapons as the weather balloon now swayed gently in the breeze two hundred feet above them.

Suddenly, a massive C-130 cargo plane, flying much too low, swooped over Lau's complex, its engines a deafening roar. The large V on its nose snagged the line stretching from the balloon, and Lau and Batman were yanked through the hole in the ceiling. The C-130 began to climb, trailing the balloon and, lower, its two human passengers—Lau screaming as he and Batman were slowly being reeled into the cargo hold of the plane.

FIFTEEN

Several hours later, James Gordon was sitting at his desk, leafing through a sheaf of reports inscribed on yellow flimsies. Detective Ramirez rapped on the open door and told Gordon there was something he'd want to see.

Gordon followed Ramirez downstairs through a throng of excited cops to the front steps of police headquarters. There, on the cement, with his hands, legs, arms, and ankles bound with thick tape, lay Lau, his eyes squeezed shut. Pinned to his chest was a sign:

Please deliver to Lieutenant Gordon.

The next two hours were busy. Lau had to be unbound, carefully, in case there was something lethal hidden on him, and examined by a physician, as well as fed, allowed to bathe, and taken to an interrogation room. Assistant District Attorney Rachel Dawes eventually entered the room, nodded to several detectives who leaned against a wall, and sat across a table from Lau.

Without preamble, Rachel said, "Give us the money, and we'll deal."

"The *money* is the only reason I'm alive," Lau said.

Rachel leaned forward. "You mean when they hear that you've helped us, they're going to kill you?"

When Lau didn't reply, Rachel stood and moved toward the door. "Enjoy your stay, Mr. Lau."

"Wait!" Lau cried, and Rachel stopped, her hand on the doorknob. "I won't give you the money, but I'll give you my clients. *All* of them."

"You were a glorified accountant," Rachel said. "What could you have on *all* of them that we could charge?"

"I'm good with calculations. I handled all their investments. One big pot."

Rachel stared at the ceiling for almost a minute, and finally said, "It might work."

On the other side of the door, Harvey Dent and James Gordon were watching the Lau interrogation on a closed-circuit television.

"You know what Miss Dawes has in mind?" Gordon asked the district attorney.

"RICO," Dent replied. "Racketeer Influenced and

Corrupt Organizations Act. If their money was pooled, we can charge all of them as one criminal conspiracy."

"Charge them with what?"

The door opened and Rachel joined them.

Dent smiled at her and continued: "In a RICO case, if we can charge *any* of the conspirators with a felony—"

"We can charge all of them with it," Rachel said.

"Want to keep going?" Dent asked Rachel.

"Love to."

"Then he's all yours."

Rachel went back into the interrogation room and stood at the table, looking down at Lau and Evans. "Mr. Lau," she said. "Do you have details of this communal fund? Ledgers, notebooks . . . ?"

Lau raised his face until he was staring into Rachel's eyes. "Immunity, protection, and a chartered plane back to Hong Kong."

"Once you've testified in open court. So with your clients locked up, what happens to the money?"

"As I said . . . I'm good with calculation."

Outside the room, Gordon looked up from the television screen. "He can't go to the county lockup. I'll keep him here in the holding cells."

"What is this, Gordon, your fortress?" Dent asked.

"You trust them over at county?"

"I don't trust them here."

"Lau stays."

"It's your call, Lieutenant. Be right."

"I am, Counselor."

SIXTEEN

Sal Maroni and the Chechen were eating rare steak in a midtown restaurant and watching a newscast on the television above the bar. The district attorney was holding a news conference on the steps of City Hall.

A reporter was speaking, ". . . Chinese government claims that its sovereign rights have been violated."

Dent's face replaced the reporter's on the screen: "I don't know about Mr. Lau's travel arrangements . . . but I'm sure glad he's back."

"I put word out," the Chechen said. "We hire the clown. He was right. We have to fix real problem. Batman." The Chechen chuckled.

The street door swung open, and James Gordon entered, a pair of handcuffs dangling from his right index finger. He sauntered over to where the Chechen and

Maroni were eating and nodded to the television. "Our boy looks good on the tube."

"You sure you want to embarrass me in front of my friend?" Maroni asked.

"Don't worry. He's coming, too. So are a lot of your other friends."

There were no buses left in the police garage that afternoon, and very few patrol cars. The men and women of Gotham's Finest were busy, arresting people in every one of the city's dozens of neighborhoods, loading them into vehicles, unloading them at stations and jails, processing them, photographing them, slamming barred doors behind them.

At four o'clock, when the courts would normally be closing for the day, the judicial session in the civic center was just getting started. A dozen newly arrested prisoners were brought before the Honorable Janet Surillo for arraignment.

The judge was reading a list of charges supplied by Harvey Dent: ". . . 849 counts racketeering, 246 counts fraud, 87 counts conspiracy murder . . ."

Judge Surillo turned a page and paused. A playing card was paper-clipped to the indictment sheet, a Joker. The judge pushed it aside with little thought as to how it got into her files, and turned her attention to the group in front of his bench.

"How do the defendants plead?"

Then there was bedlam as an army of defense lawyers all began talking at once.

Across the street, at City Hall, Harvey Dent entered the mayor's office to find Police Commissioner Loeb, Lieutenant James Gordon, and the mayor himself waiting.

"Dent!" the mayor snapped. "What the hell's going on over here?"

"I asked Lieutenant Gordon to make some arrests."

Loeb scanned a report he was holding. "Five hundred and . . ."

"Forty-nine, sir," Gordon said.

"Five hundred and forty-nine criminals at once!" the mayor shouted. "How did you convince Surillo to hear this farce?"

"She shares my enthusiasm for justice," Dent said. "After all, she is a *judge.*"

"Even if you blow enough smoke to get convictions out of Surillo," the mayor said, a bit more calmly, "you'll set a new record at appeals for the quickest kick in the ass."

"It won't matter. The head guys make bail, sure . . . but the middle-level guys, they can't, and they can't afford to be off the streets long enough for trial and appeal. They'll cut deals that include some jail time. Think of all you can do with *eighteen months* of clean streets."

The major shook his hand in the direction of Loeb

and Gordon. "I want a word alone with the district attorney."

After the door had closed, the mayor said, "The public likes you, Dent. That's the only reason this might fly. But that means it's on *you*. They're *all* coming after you now. Not just the mob . . . politicians, journalists, cops—anyone whose wallet is about to get lighter. Are you up to it? You'd better be." The mayor stood, turned, looked out a window at the now-quiet evening. "They get anything on you, those crooks will be back out on the streets, followed swiftly by you and me."

A dark shape struck the glass directly in front of the mayor's face, cracking it. Dent strode to the mayor's side, looked outside, and gasped. A man in Batman garb was dangling from a rope around his neck. He *had* to be dead. There was a playing card, a Joker, pinned to his chest with a knife.

Dent could read the writing on the card:

WILL THE REAL BATMAN PLEASE STAND UP?

It took most of the night to identify the murdered pseudo-Batman. The fingerprints weren't in the system, and nobody seemed to have a dental chart for him. At midnight, someone got around to checking the missing persons file, and there it was, the identity they'd all been seeking: Brian Douglas, late of north Gotham.

SEVENTEEN

Across town, Bruce Wayne was entering the living room of his penthouse where Alfred was arranging canapés on a sideboard. A television in the corner tuned to a newscast and turned very low.

"How's it going?" Bruce asked.

"I think your fund-raiser will be a great success, sir."

"Alfred, why do you think I wanted to hold a party for Harvey Dent?"

"I assumed it was your usual reason for socializing beyond myself and the scum of Gotham's underbelly—to try to impress Miss Dawes. Oh, and perhaps to prepare Mr. Dent for taking on that mantle you mentioned."

"Very droll. But only half-right. Actually, it's Dent. You see . . ."

Bruce's voice trailed off as something on the television

caught his attention; a Batman hanging from a rope with a question splashed across the bottom of the screen:

BATMAN DEAD?

Bruce picked up a remote and raised the volume. The image changed, from the macabre corpse to a well-coiffed anchorman who was saying: "Police released video footage found concealed on the body. Sensitive viewers be aware—it *is* disturbing."

The anchorman was gone and in his place, a badly lit picture of a blindfolded man wearing a makeshift Batman costume. The man's face beneath the mask and blindfold was bruised and bloody. He spoke in a rasp: "Name . . . Brian Douglas."

An off-screen voice: "Are you the real Batman?"

"No."

"Why do you dress up like him?"

"He's a symbol . . . that we don't have to be afraid . . . of scum like you . . ."

"But you do, Brian. You really do. You think the Batman's helped Gotham?"

Brian nodded.

"Look at me, Brian. *Look at me!*"

Brian looked up, and the camera panned from him to the Joker, in chalk white makeup, a red smear of lipstick across his scars.

The Joker cackled, and said, "*This* is how crazy Batman's made Gotham. You want order? Batman has to go. Batman has to take off his mask and turn himself in. Every day he doesn't . . . people will die. Starting tonight. I'm a man of my word."

The screen was blank for a moment, then the anchorman resumed his report. Bruce and Alfred looked at each other, but neither said a word.

Finally, Bruce asked, "Your computer setup recorded what we just saw?"

"The device would have been activated by the word 'Batman,'" Alfred replied.

"Good. Let's pull the Joker's voice from the tape. It might come in handy later."

At ten minutes after nine that night, Harvey Dent and Rachel Dawes got out of an elevator. Dent stopped, scanning the area in front of him, a lavish room almost as big as a basketball court filled with dozens of people, each wearing thousands of dollars worth of clothing and jewelry. Tuxedoed waiters circulated through the crowd offering food and drink from silver trays.

Rachel looked up at Dent. "Now I've seen it all—Harvey Dent, scourge of the underworld, scared stiff by the trust fund brigade."

Rachel waved at someone—Dent couldn't tell who—and scurried off.

Alfred appeared at Dent's elbow, holding a tray of drinks, and asked, "A little liquid courage, Mr. Dent?"

"No thanks. You're Alfred, right?"

"Yes, sir."

"Rachel talks about you all the time. You've known her her whole life?"

"Not yet, sir."

"Any psychotic ex-boyfriends I should be aware of?"

"Oh, you have *no* idea."

Alfred left Dent still standing in front of the elevators and went off to mingle with the partygoers. There was a *chup chup chup* sound that grew steadily louder, and the crowd moved to the french doors that opened onto a wide terrace. A twin-rotored helicopter descended from a cloudy sky and, with a slight shudder, came to rest on a heli-pad above the terrace. A side door slid back and Bruce Wayne, accompanied by a bevy of tall, sleek women wearing colorful cocktail dresses, crossed the terrace and entered the penthouse. He smiled and waved and when he saw Dent, still standing by the elevators, strode across the room and shook the district attorney's hand.

"Sorry I'm late," Bruce said. "Glad you started without me. Where's Rachel?"

Bruce saw Rachel talking to a woman with silver hair piled high atop her head, and raised his voice to address the room: "Rachel Dawes, my oldest friend. When she told me she was dating Harvey Dent, I had one thing to say . . . the guy from those god-awful campaign commercials?"

There was a ripple of laughter. Dent shifted his weight and stared at the floor.

" 'I believe in Harvey Dent,' " Bruce continued. The room was now quiet except for his voice. "Nice Slogan, Harvey. Certainly caught Rachel's attention. But then I started paying attention to Harvey and all he's been doing as our new DA, and you know what? *I* believe in Harvey Dent. On his watch, Gotham can feel a little safer. A little more optimistic. So get our your checkbooks and let's make sure he stays where all of Gotham wants him . . . All except the criminals, of course." Bruce took a glass from a passing waiter and raised it. "To the face of Gotham's bright future—Harvey Dent."

Dent raised his eyes and smiled at the crowd, accepting the toast.

While Bruce Wayne and Harvey Dent were basking in the approval of Gotham City's elite, James Gordon and Anna Ramirez were squinting down at a sheet of paper that lay flat on Gordon's desk.

"The card the Joker pinned to the murdered man's body," Ramirez said. "Forensics found three sets of DNA."

"Any matches?" Gordon asked.

"All three. The DNA belongs to Judge Surillo, Harvey Dent, and Commissioner Loeb."

"The Joker's telling us who he's targeting. Get a unit to Surillo's house, tell Wuertz to find Dent. Get them both into protective custody. Where's the commissioner?"

"City Hall."

"Seal the building. No one in or out till I get there."

Bruce Wayne's party was in fall swing. Most of the glittering crowd were visibly enjoying the food and drink, air-kissing casual acquaintances, gathering in knots of three or four chatting quietly or laughing. Bruce himself was on the terrace staring out at the lights of the city. Rachel Dawes passed through the French doors and joined him.

"Harvey may not know you well enough to know when you're making fun of him, but I do," Rachel said.

Bruce shook his head. "I meant every word." He moved closer to Rachel and rested his hand lightly on her shoulder. "The day you told me about, the day when Gotham no longer needs Batman . . . it's coming."

"You can't ask me to wait for that," Rachel whispered.

Bruce grasped both of Rachel's upper arms and stared down into her face. "It's happening now. Harvey is that hero. He locked up half the city's criminals, and he did it without wearing a mask. Gotham *needs* a hero with a face."

Harvey Dent moved through the glass doors and onto the terrace. His voice was jovial: "You can throw a party, Wayne, I'll give you that. Thanks again. Mind if I borrow Rachel?"

Rachel moved from Bruce to Dent and, with a single, swift backward glance, went inside.

They threaded their way through the remaining partiers, pausing to shake a hand here, speak a word there, until they reached the kitchen. Dent stood leaning against a tall, stainless-steel refrigerator, and Rachel took a place across from him, her back to a butcher block.

"You *cannot* leave me on my own with these people," he said smiling, but with an edge in his voice.

"The whole mob's after you, and you're worried about *these* guys," Rachel said, her brows rising.

"Compared to this, the mob doesn't scare me. Although I will say . . . them gunning for you makes me see things clearly."

"Oh, yeah?"

"Yeah. It makes you think about what you couldn't stand losing. And who you want to spend the rest of your life with."

"The rest of your life, huh? That's a pretty big commitment."

"Not if the mob has their way."

"Harvey, that's not funny."

"Okay, then let's be serious. What's your answer?"

Rachel lifted her chin and stared at Dent's face. "I don't have an answer."

Downtown, at City Hall, James Gordon and a retinue of detectives jostled their way through a throng of reporters and cameramen and entered the office of Commissioner Perry Loeb.

Loeb, behind his desk, looked up angrily. "Gordon, what are you playing at?"

Gordon ignored him and checked the office windows. Then he turned to the detectives who had accompanied him, and said, "We're secure. I want a floor-by-floor search of the entire building." He watched the detectives file out and turned to Loeb. "I'm sorry, sir. We believe the Joker has made a threat against your life."

"Gordon, you're unlikely to discover this for yourself, so take my word for it—the police commissioner earns a lot of threats." Loeb took a decanter half-full of amber liquid and a crystal tumbler from a drawer. "You get to explain to my wife why I'm late for dinner."

"Sir," Gordon said a bit too loudly, "the Joker card had a trace of *your* DNA on it—"

"How'd they get my DNA?" Loeb demanded.

"Somebody with access to your house or office must've lifted a tissue or a glass . . ."

Gordon stopped, then took two swift steps to the desk, reaching for the glass that Loeb was draining.

"Wait!" Gordon shouted.

But Loeb had already dropped the tumbler, spilling the liquid onto the wooden desktop which began to smoke as Loeb grabbed his throat. He made a few gurgling sounds and within seconds he was dead.

Two heavyset men in gray suits left a blue sedan illegally parked and ran up the steps of a brownstone in

Gotham Heights, a neighborhood with a reputation for bohemian that hadn't been deserved for fifty years. Judge Surillo, wearing jeans and a T-shirt, opened the door and listened as the two detectives explained why she needed protection.

"Gordon wants me to go right now?" the judge asked.

"Right now," said the first detective. "Don't bother to pack."

"These are dangerous people," said the second detective. "Even *we* don't know where you're going." He handed Surillo a sealed envelope. "This'll tell you where you're headed."

Judge Surillo, flanked by the two officers, both of whom scanned the adjoining houses and the street and were holding their pistols, went to the curb and helped the judge into the car.

"Now, let's see," Surillo said, opening the envelope with a forefinger. She pulled out a sheet of paper with a single word printed on it: UP.

Orange flame gouted from the car as it was lifted off the pavement by the force of the explosion.

There was no longer anything festive about Bruce Wayne's fund-raiser. For several minutes, the guests had been answering their cell phones or reading text messages, and their smiles were vanishing, replaced by expressions of anxiety But no one left. Apparently they believed that there was safety in numbers.

Alfred turned on the massive flat screen television and tuned it to a cable news channel. The anchorman confirmed what the partygoers already knew.

Bruce got out his cell phone and speed-dialed a number. He stepped into a spare bedroom, spoke his name and listened, then asked, "Surillo *and* Loeb?"

Meanwhile the door of the private elevator slid open, and the Joker stepped out, holding a shotgun and followed by several other armed men.

"Good evening," the Joker said, racking a shell into the gun's firing chamber. "We're the entertainment."

Rachel and Dent weren't aware of what was happening a few feet away in the living room, nor, apparently, of anything in the world except each other. They had barely moved in the five minutes since Rachel had not accepted Dent's proposal,

Dent sighed, and said, finally, "I guess no answer isn't 'no.'"

"I'm sorry, Harvey. I just—"

"It's someone else, isn't it? Just tell me it's not Wayne. The guy's a complete—"

Bruce stepped silently from behind the refrigerator. Rachel's eyes widened. She opened her mouth to say something, but Bruce was already using his fingers to press three spots on Dent's skull. Dent slumped over, and Bruce caught him.

"What are you doing?" Rachel finally managed to ask.

"They've come for him," Bruce replied, and now there was nothing of the playboy in his manner.

Bruce put Dent in a pantry closet and shoved a broom through the handles.

"Stay hidden," he told Rachel, and left the kitchen.

In the corridor outside, he met one of the Joker's thugs, who pointed a shotgun at him. Bruce wrested the weapon away from the gunman and flipped it around and hit the man with it. He fieldstripped it as he moved away, scattering the pieces.

Rachel waited only a few seconds before disobeying Bruce's order. She was not the kind of woman to remain in hiding when she might be able to *do* something. She hurried into the living room and stopped, staring at the Joker, who was sauntering among the guests.

"I have just one question," the Joker said. "Where is Harvey Dent? No answer. All righty, I'll settle for his loved ones. Any lovey-wuveys on the scene?" He looked directly at Rachel. "Hello, beautiful. You must be Harvey's squeeze, no?" He pulled a knife from under his jacket and tiptoed to Rachel's side. She stood rigid, eyes straight ahead, ignoring him. He ran his knife across her cheek. "And you *are* beautiful. You look nervous. It's the scars, isn't it? Wanna know how I got them? I had a wife, beautiful like you. Who tells me I worry too much. Who says I need to smile more. Who gambles.

And gets in *deep* with the sharks. One day they carve her face, and we've got no money for surgeries. She can't take it. I just want to see her smile again. I just want her to know that I don't care about the scars. So I put a razor in my mouth and do this to myself . . . And you know what? She can't stand the sight of me. She leaves. See, now I see the funny side. Now I'm *always* smiling."

Muted sounds were coming from his throat, and his face was contorted, but the scars made it impossible to know whether he was laughing or crying.

Bruce made his way into the master bedroom, but stopped short when he saw a couple hastily dressing themselves after enjoying each other on his bed. The couple looked embarrassed, but the man summoned enough courage to ask Bruce what was going on in the living room.

Bruce ignored him and instead walked into a closet and pulled at a false wall. As he stepped into the safe room, the female half of the couple moved swiftly toward him.

"Thank God, you've got a panic room!"

Her only reply from Bruce was the safe-room door slamming shut in her face and sealing.

Back in the living room, the Joker raised the knife from Rachel's cheek. She slugged him.

"A little fight in you," the Joker said, beaming. "I like that."

"Then you're going to love me," Batman said from behind him.

The Joker whirled and ran into Batman's fist. The knife fell to the floor, and Batman kicked it away, then spun to face two of the Joker's thugs. He pivoted on his left leg and kicked them both with his right in one continuous, sweeping motion.

The Joker tapped one ankle with the toe of the opposite foot and a blade sprung from the front of his shoe. His leg levered upward, stiffly, and the blade slid between the plates of Batman's body armor. Ignoring the wound, Batman lifted the Joker overhead and flung him across the room. There were two of the Joker's crew left standing, and both were rushing at him. He waited until they were barely a foot away before grabbing their heads and banging them together.

"Looky looky looky," the Joker sang. He had another knife pressed to Rachel's neck and held a shotgun in his other hand.

"Let her go," Batman said.

"Sure. Just take off your mask and show us all who you are . . ."

Rachel shook her head: *No!*

The Joker aimed the shotgun and blasted away the nearest windowpane. He dragged Rachel to the windowsill and nudged her over. Only the Joker's arm around her neck kept her from falling.

"Let her go," Batman repeated.

The Joker cackled. "Very poor choice of words."

He flung wide his arm and Rachel fell.

Batman straight-armed the Joker aside and dived out the window after Rachel.

She had hit a sloped glass roof belonging to the apartment below and was sliding toward the edge, her fingers unable to get purchase on the glass. Batman dove right behind her and fired his grapple, snagging Rachel's ankle as they pitched over the edge and began hurtling toward the dark street. Batman tried to get his cape stiffened so that they could glide to the street below, but only half of the cape responded. Batman grimaced and wrapped his arms around Rachel and twisted in midair so he would land first and his armor would cushion them both. They landed hard atop a taxi, rolled to the pavement, and continued rolling until they reached the sidewalk, where Batman got unsteadily to his feet, helping Rachel up as well. She was out of breath and very pale, but she gave him a smile of thanks.

Batman and Rachel stood almost completely hidden under a shop awning and watched a black SUV speed away. *Almost certainly the Joker's getaway car . . .*

"Are you all right?" Batman whispered.

Rachel said, "Let's not do that again, all right? What about Harvey—"

"He's safe."

"Thank you."

In the backseat of the SUV, the Joker was alternately gasping for breath and laughing. He touched a streamlet of blood running down his makeup-smeared chin with a forefinger, licked it, and said, "Yummy! Did you *see* that? Did you love it a great big bunch? I tossed the lovely bird into the wind and out Bats went. I wonder . . . would the Bats take a header for everyone? Or is that pretty little birdie someone *special*? Either way, we know one thing for sure now . . . Batman will always try to save the innocent. And that will be his *downfall*!"

"What about Dent?" the driver asked.

"Oh, I'm a man of my word," the Joker said, smiling.

Alfred inspected Bruce's body and found it intact. A back muscle was pulled, Bruce's left wrist sprained, but by and large he had survived the plunge from the penthouse to the street unscathed.

"Tell me," Alfred said. "When you dived out that window, did you have a plan?"

"If I'd stopped to plan, both Rachel and I would be dead. I didn't have time to do anything but *act*, and hope my reactions would be the right ones. I had to trust to the moment. It's something Rā's al Ghūl taught me."

"Just how trustworthy *is* the moment?"

Bruce laughed. "Not very. A random negative factor—a gust of wind, say—and you'd be planning my funeral."

"You seem to feel that this sort of thing might get you killed."

"This sort of thing *will* get me killed, sooner or later, if things keep going the way they are . . ."

EIGHTEEN

It was midafternoon at Gordon's office, where nobody was happy. Gordon was behind his desk talking to a stout man with bushy gray sideburns named Gerard Stephens.

"Jim, it's over!" Stephens insisted.

Gordon shook his head wearily. "As long as they don't get to Lau, we've cut off their funds."

"But the prosecution's over! No one's standing up in front of a judge while judges and police commissioners are getting blown away."

"What about Dent?"

"If he's got any sense, Dent's halfway to Mexico by now."

The door behind Stephens slammed open, and Harvey Dent strode in.

"So where do you keep your trash?" he demanded.

———

Ten minutes later, Dent and two uniformed officers entered a cell deep in Gotham Central Jail, where Lau sat on the edge of a cot.

Dent tossed a bulletproof vest at Lau. "You're due in court. I need you alive long enough to get you on record."

"No way," Lau said, laying the vest aside. "You can't protect me. You can't even protect yourselves."

Dent picked up the vest and threw it at Lau. "Refuse to cooperate on the stand, and you won't be coming back here. You'll go to county. How long do you *calculate* you'll last in *there*?"

Bruce Wayne sat in his underground lair staring at the bank of television screens. He was aware of two sets of memories, one superimposed on the other: saving a good woman, a brave and valuable woman, and years earlier using similar skills to save a man who wished to exterminate 90 percent of the world's population. What nagged at him was that he felt the same satisfaction at both rescues—saving Rachel and saving Rā's. Was there really no difference?

He heard the elevator groan to a halt behind him, and a few moments later, Alfred joined him. Bruce switched on the video equipment, and together they watched the Joker footage. Occasionally, Bruce would magnify, make louder, mute, or remove color from elements of the images, but he could get no further information from them.

He turned to Alfred. "Targeting me—Batman—won't get their money back. I knew the mob wouldn't go down without a fight, but this is different. They've crossed a line."

"You crossed it first, Master Bruce. You've hammered them, squeezed them to the point of desperation. And now, in their desperation, they've turned to a man they don't fully understand."

"Criminals aren't complicated, Alfred. We just have to figure out what he's after."

"Respectfully, Master Bruce . . . perhaps this is a man you don't understand either."

Bruce rose and went to the nearest closet.

"Allow me to bore you with a story," Alfred said. "I was in Burma. A long time ago. My friends and I were working for the local government officials. They were trying to buy the loyalty of tribal leaders, bribing them with precious stones. But their caravans were being raided in a forest north of Rangoon by a bandit. We were asked to take care of the problem, so we started looking for the stones. But after six months, we couldn't find anyone who had traded with the outlaw."

"What were you missing?"

"One day I found a child playing with a ruby as big as a tangerine. The bandit had been throwing the stones away."

"So why was he stealing them?"

"Because he thought it was good sport. Because some men aren't looking for anything logical, like money . . . they can't be bought, bullied, reasoned, or negotiated with. Some men just want to watch the world burn."

Bruce nodded and reached into a cabinet to get one of his Batman suits.

"Where to tonight, Master Bruce? The opera? An ice-cream social, perhaps?"

Bruce was snapping armor into place. "I think I'll sniff around the city . . . or maybe the *top* of the city."

Ten minutes later, Batman stood atop a skyscraper, listening.

At this early hour of the morning, the neighborhood around Eighth and Orchard, in what had once been the city's retail center, was all but deserted. James Gordon had no trouble racing his unmarked sedan down the narrow streets, leading three patrol cars whose sirens were howling. Gordon braked to a screeching halt at the intersection and before his engine had stopped growling, he and Ramirez were racing into a tenement building, weapons out, followed by six uniformed cops. Gordon kicked open the door to apartment four. He holstered his gun. He was in a cramped kitchen with a bathtub partly covered by a shower curtain against one bare brick wall. In the center of the room, two dead men sat at a table covered with oilcloth. Each was holding five cards, all jokers, and each was disfigured by crude leers carved into their faces. Both had driver's licenses pinned to their shirts.

"Get downstairs," Gordon told the cops. "Secure the area and somebody get a medical examiner down here."

The cops left, and someone spoke from behind the shower curtain. "Check the names."

Gordon bent over and peered at the drivers licenses. "Patrick *Harvey*. Richard *Dent*."

"Harvey Dent," Ramirez said.

Batman stepped from behind the curtain. "I need ten minutes with the scene before your men contaminate it."

"*Us* contaminate it?" Ramirez asked angrily. "It's because of you that these guys are dead in the first place."

"Ramirez," Gordon warned.

Batman moved past the bodies to a small pock in the wall. He removed a knife with a needle blade from his belt and began digging. He twisted the knife and caught a bullet fragment in his palm.

"That's brick," Gordon said. "You're gonna try and take ballistics off a shattered bullet?"

"No," Batman said. "Fingerprints."

"He's not serious," Ramirez muttered.

"Whatever you're gonna do," Gordon said, "do it fast. He has another target."

Gordon pointed to a *Gotham Times* obituary dated with tomorrow's date folded underneath Dent's arm. It read: "Mayor Anthony Garcia was shot and killed today by the criminal mastermind known as the Joker. Surgeons at Gotham General confirmed that Mayor Garcia had succumbed to massive internal bleeding caused by rounds from a high-powered rifle. The mayor was forty years old." Garcia's photo had a red *Xo Xo* written next to it, and in the same red, all over the obituary, was scrawled: HA HA HA.

Lucius Fox had heard the news about the early-morning murders on his car radio as he was driving in to work and knew he probably wouldn't be seeing his boss that day, which was okay; the day looked to be extremely routine except for a ten o'clock appointment with the lawyer, Coleman Reese.

Reese was right on time and looked a bit excited.

"What can I do for you?" Fox asked him.

"You asked me to do the diligence on the L.S.I. Holdings deal again. I found some irregularities."

"Well, their CEO *is* in police custody."

"Not with their numbers. With *yours*. A whole division of Wayne Enterprises disappeared overnight. So I went down to the archives and started pulling old files." Reese removed a blueprint from his attaché case, unfolded it, and pushed it across the desk to Fox. "My kids love the Batman. I thought he was pretty cool, too. Out there, kicking some ass."

Fox looked briefly at the blueprint. Across the top at one corner was scrawled: the Tumbler.

"Changes things when you know it's just a rich kid

trying to play dress-up," Reese continued. Reese pointed to Fox's initials in the approval box. "Your project. Don't tell me you don't recognize your baby pancaking cop cars on the evening news. Now you're getting sloppy. Applied Sciences was a small, dead department—who'd notice? But now you've got the entire R&D department burning cash, claiming its related to *cell phones* for the Army. What are you building him now, a rocket ship? I want ten million a year, for the rest of my life."

Fox folded the blueprint and contemplated Reese. "Let me get this straight. You think that your client, one of the wealthiest and most powerful men in the world, is secretly a vigilante who spends his nights beating criminals to a pulp with his bare hands. And now your plan is to blackmail this person?"

Reese stared at Fox, who was smiling lazily.

"Good luck," Fox drawled.

Coleman Reese left Fox angry and insulted. Blackmail? No. Blackmailers were criminals, and Coleman was no criminal. He was a lawyer, one who had not been given his due. He had been cheated. His talents were neither recognized nor rewarded. He had been recruited from the graduating class of Gotham University's law school with promises of quick promotion and financial largesse. Five years had passed—five whole years!—and where was he? Stuck in a Wayne Enterprises law library doing due diligence. Oh, the money was all right, he guessed;

the starting salary had been pretty good, the cost-of-living raises had come promptly, and once he had even been given a bonus that financed a nice vacation in the south of France. But a man of his abilities should *not* be stuck doing chores in libraries. He should be in a courtroom, where his eloquence and, yes, his personal charm and charisma would not only be winning cases, but would be putting the best possible face on Wayne Enterprises.

He was not done with Lucius Fox or, for that matter, with Bruce Wayne.

Bruce and Alfred were busy testing firearms. Earlier, Bruce had fired a rifle in his underground chamber while Alfred stood on the ground above. As they had suspected, the sound of the shot was not audible outside the bunker. Now, Alfred was handing Bruce a bullet inscribed with a grid. Bruce slid it into an ammunition clip and the clip into a computer-controlled Gatling gun. He and Alfred put on ear protectors, and Bruce thumbed a button. The gun hummed and began dollying sideways and spinning and blasting slugs into a series of identical brick wall samples. When the gun stopped firing, Bruce went to the bricks, carrying the slug he had found at the Orchard Street murders. He held the slug up to each of the newly made holes in the walls, then selected two of the bricks and took them to an x-ray scanner. He toggled a switch and high-resolution, three-dimensional images of the bullet fragments lit up the screen.

An hour later, Bruce was standing next to Lucius Fox at the Applied Sciences Division of Wayne Enterprises. They were standing in front of another screen, and Fox was saying, "Here's your original scan and"—he pushed a button and a second image appeared on the screen—"here it is reverse-engineered."

Fox pushed another button, and the images began moving, seeming to assemble themselves into whole bullets. Finally, the movement stopped; one of the images bore an array of swirling lines.

"And *here*," Bruce said, "is a thumb print."

"I'll make you a copy," Fox said. "Mr. Wayne, did you assign R&D?"

"Yes, government telecommunications project."

"I wasn't aware we had any new government contracts. Can you—"

"Lucius, I'm playing this one pretty close to the vest."

"Fair enough."

Fox removed a copy of the thumbprint taken from the shattered bullet and handed it to Bruce. "Now, what about the matter of Mr. Reese I told you about when I called?"

Alfred was waiting for his boss in the bunker, killing time by watching a cooking show on television. Alfred greeted him and watched as Bruce fed the thumbprint into a slot on one of the computers.

Alfred sat in front of a keyboard and, looking over his shoulder, said, "I'll run it through all the databases."

"Cross-reference the addresses. Look for Parkside and around there."

While Alfred busied himself, Bruce went into the shadows and returned wheeling a motorcycle, an MV Augusta Brutale, which he pushed onto the elevator.

"Got one," Alfred said. "Melvin White, aggravated assault, moved to Arkham Asylum twice. He's at 1502 Randolph, just off State Apartment."

"Overlooking the funeral procession," Bruce said, climbing onto the motorcycle. "Not good."

NINETEEN

It was the day of Commissioner Loeb's funeral. Not everyone had liked the commissioner, and he had certainly had his share of political enemies, but he was a Gothamite, his death had been unjust and untimely, and respect was his due. Just after sunrise, people began gathering along the curbs or staking out space in windows above the streets, some with folding chairs, some with picnic coolers full of snacks, many wearing black armbands. It seemed like everyone had their hands folded, their eyes staring at the ground.

Except, maybe, the police.

The event had been happening for about an hour. The marchers had traveled less than a mile. For some, this was their moment, their chance to show the world that they were good citizens, decent folk who honored the dead. The police presence was very visible. There was the GCPD marching band, of course, and hundreds of uniforms on the sidewalks and standing in the gutters and directing traffic at intersections. There were an equal number of *non*uniformed officers pretending to watch the funeral and really watching everything else. And high above, on the rooftops, tight-lipped men in fatigues peered through the scopes of sniper rifles.

Gordon, standing on a corner, keyed his radio, and growled, "How's it look on top?"

One of the snipers, a twenty-year veteran, Sergeant Raphael Mayer, keyed his own radio, and replied: "We're tight. But frankly . . . there's a *lot* of windows."

Gordon looked up at the sun glaring off thousands of glass panes. Yeah, a lot of windows, all right.

Negotiating the streets of Gotham would have been impossible in a car, jammed as they were with mourners. But driving his motorcycle, Bruce could weave and turn and, quite quickly, get to where he was going. And if anyone recognized him? If he had been Batman, everyone would have noticed, followed him, tried to stop him. But Bruce Wayne? Hey, it's just billionare Bruce up to one of his usual tricks.

He braked in an alleyway between two medium-sized apartment buildings a dozen yards from a parade barrier. He dismounted, grabbed the lowest rung of a fire escape ladder, pulled himself upward. He continued on to the fifth landing. It took him only moments to open a window and begin stalking down a dimly lit corridor. He counted doors until he reached one marked: 1502.

He pressed his ear against the wood paneling and heard a voice—muffled and booming at once. The mayor's voice. His honor must be making his standard fallen comrades speech in the street directly outside the building:

. . . and as we recognize the sacrifice of this brave servant, we must remember that vigilance is the price of . . .

The same old speech, the collection of clichés the guy mouthed every time a cop or a fireman or a politician died. But if Bruce were right about what was inside apartment 1502, it would be the mayor's *last* speech. Unless he acted.

He emptied his mind of expectation and speculation, because as Rā's had taught him, he had to put himself fully in the present moment when going into combat. He kicked in the door and dived and rolled and—

A sniper scope on a tripod at the window. On the floor, eight men, arms and legs and mouths wrapped in tape. Bruce went to the nearest one and pulled the tape from his lips.

Gasping, the man said, "They took our guns . . . our uniforms . . ."

Guns and . . . *uniforms*?

Bruce sprang to the window and looked through the scope to see:

The mayor. His honor guard, eight uniformed men who were raising their rifles, aiming at the mayor. Through the round lens, Bruce could see a face he thought he recognized, the hollowed eyes and gruesome scars . . .

Gordon saw the scarred face, too, and for a few seconds tried to place the man's face. Then he realized that the man's rifle was out of sync. Seconds later he jumped as the rifles fired. Slugs slammed into his back as Gordon lurched into the mayor, and the two men tumbled to the pavement.

On the rooftop across the street, Sergeant Raphael Mayer heard shots and saw through his scope sunlight glancing off a similar scope in a fifth-floor window. He squeezed the trigger of his weapon.

The street was pandemonium: shouts, screams, the merrymakers now a mindless mob, desperately afraid, running mindlessly, seeking any kind of safety. Two of the patrolmen had the presence of mind to shoot at the murderous honor guard. One of the shots found a target, the leg of an honor guardsmen, who groaned, dropped his rifle, and folded to the ground.

———

Sergeant Mayer's slugs shattered the upper pane of the window and, as Bruce rolled away, splintered the window frame. He scanned the room to be certain that the bound men—the real honor guard—were out of the line of fire, then sprinted into the corridor.

Harvey Dent had been with Rachel Dawes at the podium, standing behind Mayor Garcia along with a dozen other dignitaries, when the gunfire began. He pushed Rachel down and told her to stay put, then jumped from the platform and ran forward. The crowd, still mostly confused and in panic, made progress difficult: he was elbowed and jostled, and twice he fell. It took him several minutes to reach the area where the violence had occurred. He saw an ambulance parked in an alleyway between two buildings. He trotted to the ambulance and slipped through the open doors. Inside, the phony guardsman who had been shot was sitting on the edge of a gurney. A paramedic winding a bandage around his leg and two uniformed cops stood nearby, their heads bowed under the low roof.

Dent crouched by the guardsman. "Tell me what you know about the Joker."

The man smirked. Then Dent noticed the name tag on his uniform: *Officer Rachel Dawes*.

Dent glanced past the guardsman and saw through a small window that the driver's seat was empty, and the keys were in the ignition. He told the cops to be sure the area was secure, and after they'd gone, he circled to the front of the ambulance, got in, and drove away.

Clara Street, near the city limits, was a crowded block in a poor state, with run-down buildings, broken sidewalks, and very little green where the neighborhood's children could play. The Gordon house was a modest building in the middle of the block. Barbara Gordon stood speechless on the run-down front porch as Officer Gerard Stephens tried to console her.

"I'm sorry, Barbara," Stephens said, placing a hand on her shoulder.

Barbara brushed it off and stepped past Stephens. She looked out in the dark and shouted, "Are you there? Are you? You brought this on us. *You did! You* brought this . . ." Her voice caught, she sobbed, and collapsed into Stephens's arms.

Batman was nearby. He hung his head.

It was dark in Gotham City by eight, and the streets were emptier than usual. All civic events and most theater and musical performances had been canceled following the afternoon's shooting. The movie houses and multiplexes and nightclubs were still open, and a few citizens were inside them, determined to be amused no matter how far into despair everyone else had fallen.

At police headquarters, all of the Gotham City Major Crimes Unit stood next to the searchlight, its beam vanishing into a cloudless sky.

"Let's switch it off," Officer Stephens said. "He ain't coming. He doesn't want to talk to us. God help whomever he *does* want to talk to."

TWENTY

Salvatore Maroni fancied himself an old-time kind of guy—an old-fashioned crime boss, a mobster with class. He liked flash: flashy clothes, flashy cars, flashy woman, and flashy clubs. Tonight, he was in one of his favorite haunts, a nightclub near the waterfront, a joint he considered a lot classier than the dumps the Chechen owned. He was sitting in a booth next to his newest flashy woman and his bodyguards, listening to music with a beat a man could feel in the pit of his stomach, watching dancers whom he saw in half-second intervals because, just now, the entire place was lit by strobes.

"Can't we go someplace quieter?" the flashy woman shouted. "We can't hear each other talk."

"I don't wanna hear you talk," Maroni shouted back.

He leaned back to watch the dancers on the floor

below, visible in half-second bursts of brightness filled with human motion.

Two men with assault rifles were on the catwalk above the dance floor and across from Maroni's table, gazing down at the moving bodies, charged with watching for trouble. They didn't see a skylight open behind them, nor the figure that seemed to congeal from the night. The bigger of the two felt a breeze on the back of his neck and was turning when a fist caught him beneath the chin. His partner caught a glimpse of him falling in a burst of light and was raising his weapon when something struck him behind the ear. His gun slipped from his hand and fell onto the catwalk. One of Maroni's bodyguards reacted immediately, jerking a pistol from beneath his jacket and running onto the catwalk.

A burst of light: a silhouette dropping from the catwalk.

Darkness.

Light: A caped figure standing in front of the bodyguard.

Darkness.

Light: the bodyguard collapsing.

Darkness.

Light: Maroni half-out of his seat, gun in hand, eyes wide.

Darkness.

Light: Batman was crouching on the table, his hands

on Maroni, his teeth clenched, and his mask a devil's face.

Darkness.

For Rachel Dawes, the day had been hellish, and now the evening was becoming the same. She hated funerals, hated displaying herself, and had agreed to take part only to please Harvey Dent. Then the gunfire, the panic, the stampede . . . She had gotten herself out of the thick of it, had learned from a cop with a radio what had happened, had walked downtown to her office at the courthouse, where she might be of some use to somebody. The situation was chaotic there, too, but she had managed to organize the deployment of the junior prosecutors and was beginning to deal with the interns when her cell phone rang.

"Harvey, where are you?" she asked, her voice rising above the din around her.

"Where are *you*?"

"Where *you* should be, at Major Crimes, trying to sort through—"

"Rachel, listen to me. You're not safe there."

"This is Gordon's unit, Harvey."

"Gordon's dead, Rachel."

"They didn't tell me that. He vouched for the honor guard . . ."

"He's gone. And the Joker's named you next."

Rachel gazed around the room, at the people she knew and the people she didn't. There were a lot of the latter.

"Rachel, I can't let anything happen to you," Dent said. "I love you too much. Is there someone—*anyone*—in this city we can trust?"

"Bruce. We can trust Bruce Wayne."

"Rachel, I know he's your friend, but—"

"Trust me, Harvey. Right now, Bruce's penthouse is the safest place in the city."

"Okay. Go straight there. Don't tell anyone where you're going. I'll meet you there. I love you."

Harvey Dent hung up the phone and turned to a man with a bandage on his leg and duct tape on his wrists and ankles. Then he started the ambulance up again and drove east.

When Sal Maroni finally opened his eyes, he didn't know where he was or what had happened, not at first. Then the masked face swam into his vision—the Batman. The vigilante must have knocked him out in the club.

"I want the Joker," Batman growled.

Maroni twisted around to get a better look at where he was. A fire escape. Outside the club, probably, one floor up.

"From one professional to another," Maroni said, "if you're trying to scare someone, pick a better spot. From this height, the fall wouldn't kill me."

"I'm counting on it."

Batman released Maroni, who fell hard to the sidewalk and yelped.

In a moment, Batman was beside him. "Where is he?"

"I don't know," Maroni said from between clenched teeth. "He found *us*."

"He must have friends."

"Friends? You met this guy?"

"*Someone* knows where he is."

Batman grasped Maroni's collar and hauled him back up the fire escape.

Maroni looked at him and sneered. "No one's gonna tell you anything. They're wise to your act—you got *rules* . . . The Joker, he's got no rules. No one's gonna cross him for you. You want this guy, you got one way. And you already know what that is. Just take off that mask and let him come find you. Or you want to let a couple more people get killed while you make up your mind?"

Batman dropped Maroni again and listened to him yell.

Dent drove until he found what he was looking for, an underground parking garage with an automated ticket dispenser and no attendant in sight. He guided the ambulance down the winding ramp until he stopped on the bottom of the structure, away from security cameras. He went to the rear of the ambulance, searched the bound man's pockets, and found an address.

Dent then pulled a .38 revolver from his coat pocket and was holding it inches from the bound man's nose.

"I didn't find anything useful around here," he said. "But I *will* get information. Count on it."

The man spat at Dent.

"You want to play games?" Harvey asked. He showed the man a handful of cartridges and fed them into the gun. He snapped the magazine closed and rammed the gun barrel hard against the man's temple, then pivoted it an inch and fired. The sound was loud in the filthy basement, and the slug pocked the wall behind the bound man's ear.

The man's eyes were wide, his voice unsteady. "You wouldn't . . ."

Dent stepped back and took his lucky coin from his pocket. "No, I wouldn't. That's why I'm not going to leave it up to me." Dent held the coin in front of the man's eyes. "Heads—you get to keep your head. Tails . . . not so lucky. So, you want to tell me about the Joker?"

The man lowered his eyes, bit his lip, said nothing. Dent flipped the coin, caught it, slapped it on the back of the hand that was holding the gun. Heads.

"Go again?" Dent asked pleasantly.

"I don't *know* anything," the man blurted.

Dent flipped the coin, but did not catch it. Batman did that.

"You'd leave a man's life to chance?" Batman asked Dent.

"Not exactly."

"His name's Thomas Schiff. He's a paranoid schizo-phrenic, a former patient at Arkham Asylum. The kind of mind the Joker attracts. What did you expect to learn from him?"

"The Joker killed Gordon and . . . and Loeb. He's go-ing to kill *Rachel* . . ."

"You're the symbol of hope that I could never be. Your stand against organized crime is the first legitimate ray of light in Gotham for decades. If anyone saw this, every-thing would be undone, all the criminals you got off the streets would be released. And Jim Gordon will have died for nothing." Batman handed the coin to Dent. "You're going to call a press conference. Tomorrow morning."

"Why?"

"No one else will die because of me. Gotham is in your hands now."

"You can't. You can't give in."

But Batman was gone.

It was almost 4:00 A.M. when Bruce Wayne finally got back to his penthouse. He saw light under the door of the guest bedroom and knocked softly on the door.

Rachel Dawes told him to come in.

She was sitting on a window seat, staring out at the silhouetted buildings all around, still dressed in her work clothes. She glanced up at Bruce. "Harvey called. He says Batman is going to turn himself in."

"I have no choice."

"You honestly think it's going to stop the Joker from killing?"

"Perhaps not. But I've got enough blood on my hands. I've seen, now, what I would have to become to stop men like him—what I've already become. Last night, I tortured Maroni. The end never justifies that kind of means."

Bruce stopped talking and looked past Rachel, out the window. Finally, he said, "You once told me that if the day came when I was *finished* . . . we'd be together."

"Bruce, don't make me your one hope for a normal life."

Bruce moved next to her. "But did you mean it?"

"Yes."

Their faces moved close together, and for a moment, Rachel laid her cheek against Bruce's. Their lips touched, tentatively at first, then passionately.

They remained locked in the kiss for a full minute before Rachel pulled away, and said, "But they won't let us be together after you turn yourself in."

Bruce said nothing. He stepped closer to Rachel. She put her hands on his shoulders and gently pushed him away.

"All right," he murmured.

He went to the door, reaching for the knob. He hesitated, turned to look sadly at Rachel over his shoulder, then left the room.

He went into his own bedroom and lay on top of the covers, lost in thought and feeling melancholy. Eventually, he drifted off to a fitful sleep. Although he knew that he must dream—every sane person did—he usually did not remember his dreams. This night—morning, really—was an exception. He saw his father, not dressed as he had been the night he'd been murdered, not dressed for the opera, but as he used to dress for work, in a doctor's white jacket with a stethoscope around his neck, and he was frowning, obviously angry, shouting words Bruce could not hear, but somehow understood anyway, words about means and ends and becoming what one beheld . . .

Bruce awoke with a start, the question ringing in his mind: *Have I become what I beheld? Really? And if I have, what am I? A fighter for justice, the salvation of my city, a bulwark, a hero, a champion . . . Or an egoist who enjoys dominating people weaker than I am? Is my whole crusade against crime just an excuse? Everything I said to Dent was true, I must put an end to it. Dent needs to become Gotham's true hero, not me . . .*

When Alfred arrived in the bunker later that morning, Bruce gave him instructions, and they began to feed documents into an incinerator. Alfred paused, looking down at a book. "Even the diaries?"

"Anything that could lead back to Lucius or Rachel."

Alfred tossed the book into the incinerator and looked questioningly at Bruce.

"What would you have me do, Alfred? People are dying. What would you have me do?"

"Endure, Master Bruce. Take it. They'll hate you for it, but that's the point of Batman . . . he can be the outcast. He can make the choice no one else will face. The right choice."

Bruce shook his head. "Today I've found out what Batman can't do. He can't endure *this*. Today you get to say I told you so."

Alfred looked sadly at his master. "Today I don't want to."

Rachel went into the guest bedroom. She *had* to get some sleep. She lay fully dressed on top of the bedspread and closed her eyes. A clock ticked, and she could hear the distant murmur of the traffic in the street below.

Suddenly, her eyes opened and she swung her legs over the side of the bed, stood, hurried to a small desk in the corner. She switched on a light, sat, and found a pen and a sheaf of notepaper in a drawer.

Dear Bruce,

She began writing, quickly, not rereading, not pausing, her need to get everything on paper too urgent.

Rachel was exhausted and worried. She rejoined Alfred in the living area and had a sandwich of salmon and French bread and some kind of fantastic coffee, then sat with Alfred at the kitchen counter, nibbling and sipping and watching a press conference on television. The camera zoomed in on Harvey Dent, standing on the steps of City Hall, surrounded by reporters, who were thrusting microphones at him.

". . . but that's not why we're demanding he turn himself in," Dent was saying. "We're doing it because we're scared. We've been happy to let Batman clean up our streets for us until now—"

"Things are worse than ever," someone yelled from the crowd.

"Yes, they are. But the night is darkest just before the dawn. And I promise you, the dawn *is* coming. One day, Batman will have to answer for the laws he's broken—but to *us*, not to this madman."

A uniformed police sergeant yelled, "No more dead cops." Several of his fellow officers echoed him.

Another group, citizens this time, began to chant, "Where *is* the Batman?"

The chanting stopped. Bruce Wayne, standing at the rear of the crowd, began inching forward.

Dent shrugged. "So be it." He turned to the knot of police standing on the steps behind him. "Take the Batman into custody."

Bruce continued to move determinedly forward.

"*I* am the Batman," Harvey Dent proclaimed.

Rachel watched Dent being handcuffed on television.

She turned to Alfred. "Why is he letting Harvey do this?"

"I don't know. He went down to the press conference and—"

"Just stood by!"

"Perhaps both Bruce and Mr. Dent believe that Batman stands for something more important than a terrorist's whims, Miss Dawes, even if everyone hates him for it. That's the sacrifice he's making—not to be a hero. To be something more."

"Well, you're right about one thing—letting Harvey take the fall is not heroic." Rachel handed an envelope to Alfred. "You know Bruce best, Alfred . . . give it to him when the time is right."

"How will I know?"

"It's not sealed."

Rachel kissed Alfred's cheek. "Good-bye, Alfred."

"Good-bye, Rachel."

The Major Crimes Unit was unusually busy that night. Cops who were off duty hung around because . . . well, it had been a hell of a day and maybe something else might happen, and even if nothing did, there were worse ways to kill a night than drinking coffee and talking.

A number of cops she'd worked with called greetings to Rachel as she passed through the bullpen and descended the steel steps to the lockup.

Harvey Dent, in a small cell, seemed to be waiting for her. He smiled at her through the bars, and said, "I'm sorry I didn't have time to talk this through with you."

"I know what you're doing, Harvey."

"They're transferring me to central holding. This is the Joker's chance. When he attacks, the Batman will take him down."

"No! This is too dangerous . . . Don't offer yourself as bait!"

A uniformed guard, flanked by two others, told Dent it was time to go and unlocked the cell door. The guards handcuffed Dent and locked shackles around his ankles, then marched him outside. Nobody seemed to care that Rachel was following. Hampered by the shackles, Dent was taking half steps and Rachel had no trouble keeping pace with him.

"He's using you as bait," she said. "But he doesn't know if he can get the Joker. He's failed so far."

"How do you know what the Batman's thinking?" Dent asked.

"I just do, okay, Harvey? This isn't just about you. What about all the people counting on you to turn this city around? Tell everyone the truth—"

Awkwardly, because of the handcuffs, Dent removed his lucky coin from a hip pocket. "Heads I go through with it."

"Harvey, this is your *life*. You don't leave something like this to chance . . ."

Dent tossed the coin to her. Rachel caught it and looked: Heads.

"I'm not leaving anything to chance," Dent said.

Rachel turned the coin over. The reverse side was heads, too.

The guards loaded Dent into the back of a transport van and closed the doors behind him.

"You make your own luck," Rachel murmured.

During his wild years, roaming the globe, often in the company of thieves and killers, Bruce had often done things he considered shameful. But none of those ugly deeds approached what he was doing now, using a good man as a pawn in a game that might end in death.

If all went well—if all went *half*-well—the Joker would attack Dent and Batman would attack the Joker and by tomorrow this whole thing would be finished and everyone could get on with their lives.

Bruce didn't expect to avoid punishment entirely; he *had* played fast and loose with the city's laws, and in the process endangered innocent lives. But he could hope that a judge or jury would see that he had acted in the best interests of his fellow citizens and the city he loved, and be lenient. A big fine, a few months in a minimum-security facility, maybe just community service. Community service—that would be ironic; he planned to devote the rest of his life to serving the community and would welcome an early start as part of the price he had to pay.

First, however, was the Joker. That lunatic had become his priority, more important to him than the mob, the corruption, any of it. The Joker had killed Loeb. The Joker had tried to kill Harvey Dent and was going to try for Rachel next. The Joker *had* to be stopped. By any means necessary . . .

TWENTY-ONE

It was something rarely seen on city streets, a convoy, with two patrol cars leading the armored van, followed by two SWAT vans, all speeding down a freeway, past road-blocks that denied traffic access from side streets and on-ramps. Suddenly, a truck lumbered to a stop at an intersection where a police officer was holding up traffic.

The cop ran from his post at one of the barricades and approached the cab. "You wait like everyone else," he told the driver, then died from a shotgun blast.

A second truck pulled off the exit ramp and stopped in the middle of the avenue, a bright red fire department hook-and-ladder. A minute later, it burst into flame, completely blocking both sides of the freeway and isolating the middle and rear of the convoy.

In the cab of the armored car, the driver and his companion were listening to words crackling from the radio: "All units be advised. Obstruction ahead. All units will exit down to lower Fifth."

"Lower Fifth?" the SWAT officer riding shotgun muttered. "We'll be like ducks in a barrel down there."

The convoy left the freeway by the nearest ramp and rolled through the underground highway. A garbage truck casually swiped the rear vehicles of the convoy off the road, and from there chaos erupted.

"Get us out of here," the SWAT officer said as the garbage truck filled the rearview mirror. "We've got company back there!"

Both men were knocked for a loop as the garbage truck rammed the car's rear bumper, smashing it forward.

At the head of the convoy, a second truck smashed into the SWAT van, smashing it through the concrete barrier on the side of the road and into the river. The truck then pulled alongside the armored car. The driver could see that the LAUGHTER IS THE BEST MEDICINE logo on the side had a crude "S" painted next to it so that it now read SLAUGHTER, along with "HA HA HA" repeated all along the side.

A second later the side door slid open to reveal the Joker brandishing a machine gun. The armored car locked its brakes, but the garbage truck attached to it from behind kept pushing it forward. The Joker fired the gun with abandon, bullets riddling the side of the armored car.

Inside the van, the guards flinched at the bullet fire and lifted their guns as Harvey Dent sat calmly in the midst of the pandemonium.

The Joker dropped the machine gun and picked up an RPG, but stopped before firing at the driver of the armored car. Instead, he stared behind him as the Batmobile raced toward the garbage truck attached to the armored car.

Seconds later, it plowed into the garbage truck, throwing it up into the concrete ceiling. The Batmobile continued forward on its own momentum as the garbage truck came apart behind it, then whipped around and headed back to the armored car.

Inside the Batmobile, Batman shook his head and heard the vehicle's computer speaking to him: *Damage catastrophic. Initiate eject and self-destruct.*

Batman adjusted his position in the seat and hit a button. Armed guards grabbed at Batman's forearms as explosive bolts fired all around the pod.

The Joker and his driver looked back at the Batmobile, a huge grin on his face.

"Is that *him*?" the driver gasped.

"*Anyone* could be driving that thing," the Joker said. "Stay on Dent."

The Joker lined up his RPG and aimed at the armored car. He fired as the armored car began braking. The RPG slammed into the squad car in front of the armored car, and the squad car exploded. The armored van kept on going, and the Batmobile sped up to join the pursuit.

As the Joker turned the RPG toward the armored car and fired, the Batmobile crashed down in the open space between them and took the hit. The rocket struck the Batmobile's rear and exploded. Fire bathed the street and the Batmobile crashed through a retaining wall and landed in an access road alongside the underground highway. For a moment, the air seemed to be filled with spinning shards of dark metal as the Tumbler disintegrated. One of these shards smashed through the driver's side window of the Joker's truck and buried itself in the driver's head, killing him.

Inside the Batmobile, Batman wrestled with the pod controls as the car somersaulted across the street. It came to rest against one of the pillars supporting the overpass, a tangled heap of smoking metal, its rear wheels scattered across the roadway.

The Joker jumped down from the truck and looked back at the burning wreckage of the Batmobile. Giggling, he yanked the dead driver from behind the wheel of the cab and took his place. With a quick shift of gears, he pulled back onto the roadway in pursuit of the armored car.

Inside the Batmobile, the computer spoke a final time: *good-bye*.

Panels blew out from the front of the Batmobile and, a few seconds later, Batman was hoisted up and out over the front wheel, then the pod pushed the other wheel in front to form what appeared to be a motorcycle. He shot forward from the wreckage just as what was left of the Batmobile detonated and erupted into a massive fireball.

Now a block away, Batman glanced back at the conflagration, confident that any clue to his identity and any technology that might be useful to the Joker or anyone else would be destroyed.

He drove through the access corridor of the highway. He sped past cars at a stoplight, then, realizing his progress was blocked by a line of parked cars. He began firing the pod guns at them, destroying the vehicles one by one.

Richard and Raymond Peterson were bored of sitting in traffic. They had been stuck in the back of their parents' station wagon for almost forty minutes, and were trying to keep themselves amused. Turning to look at the row of parked cars not too far behind them, they aimed their fingers at them, pretending to blow them up.

Loud explosions soon drowned the noises they made out as one by one the cars they were pretending to shoot started blowing up! Just as the two boys were trying to figure things out, the dark shape of Batman speeding over the remaining cars on his pod filled the rear window.

"Whoa! The Batman!" shouted Raymond.

"No way," said Richard. "Cool!"

Above, men in a helicopter were obeying a guess from their commander and pursuing a truck traveling much faster than it should have been. Down a city street about a mile from a densely populated suburb and a sprawling shopping mall that served it and those Gothamites who didn't mind a little ride.

"Be bad if he gets to those civilians," the pilot said.

"Then we won't let 'im," his companion said, cocking an assault rifle.

Rachel had gone back to her office, and was sitting slumped in her chair, listening to a portable radio and watching a television with the sound muted. Both were reporting on the violence in lower Gotham, and both had, really, nothing to say. The police had decreed the air over the area a no-fly zone and patrol cars were blocking land access. All the journalists could say was that *something* was going on and that something was noisy.

The Joker was alternately watching the chopper directly overhead and the pavement in front of him. The sky was almost completely dark, but the chopper's red running lights betrayed its position and the truck's head beams lit the road. The Joker braked the truck, pulled a walkie-talkie from the dashboard and shouted into it: "Tee 'em up."

On a nearby rooftop, a thickset man wearing coveralls aimed a cable gun, a twin to the one used in the bank robbery—

And another man, on a fire escape, also in coveralls, aimed a cable gun—

Both guns discharged at once, and both struck the seventh floor of an office building, forming an X over the street, nearly invisible against the night sky and the shadows cast by the buildings.

At the last second, the helicopter pilot saw the cables, but by then his rotor had struck the place where they crossed. The chopper's nose tilted up, and then down, as it dropped toward a nearby building, then crashed to the street. The engine exploded, scattering fiery debris into the air.

Batman steered the pod across three lanes of traffic and into the parking lot that adjoined the commuter station. He crashed through the front doors and was in a long mall lined with specialty shops. He gunned the pod up a steep flight of steps and exited his shortcut.

Dozens of commuters stopped staring down the tracks, looking for their train, and looked instead at something they had never seen before, some kind of motorcycle and . . . Could that possibly be the *Batman* astride it?

He saw the Joker's truck on a side street directly behind the tracks and gunned the pod's engine, bouncing off the platform and across two sets of rails and up onto another platform and down steps and onto the street, a half block from the truck. Batman spotted a possible shortcut, which might put him ahead of the Joker, a narrow alley that bisected the block. But six Dumpsters were stacked at the far end, completely blocking the egress onto the street. Without slowing, Batman thumbed a red button on the pod's handlebars and the cannons from beside the front wheel fired. There were two blasts, two burst of red flame, and, with a deafening *clang*, the Dumpsters tumbled out of the way.

The Joker slowed as he saw, through the grimy windshield, the pod and Batman emerge from the fire and dust a block ahead. The pod was skidding impossibly sideward, still racing toward them.

"Guess it *was* him," he said admiringly.

The pod was equipped with state-of-the-art weaponry, and one device might do the trick . . . He touched a stud on the steering gear and a harpoon trailing a steel line left the front of the pod with a loud *hissss* . . . It embedded itself below the bumper, then Batman swerved underneath the truck, slalomed, and guided the pod around a light pole several times as the line between axle and pole tautened. As the cable went taut, it ripped one of the posts from its foundations. The truck's front wheels caught, and it flipped over end over end.

The Joker kicked out a badly cracked window and crawled from the wreckage. He jumped over the median and began waving his pistol at oncoming traffic.

Batman released the end of the cable and gunned his engine, ramping up a building at the end of the street, tilting the pod up and over. The carriage of the pod spun around so that when the pod landed, Batman was upright and facing the street. He then guided the pod up and over the median and past cars whose drivers were gawking. Batman sped toward the Joker, who was firing randomly at the oncoming traffic. As he saw Batman approach, he started walking calmly toward him.

"Hit me. Come on. *Hit me!*" he shouted at Batman as he held out his arms. He knew that Batman would never kill anyone, but he also knew that same rule might not apply to him. He watched in satisfaction as the pod did not alter its course and Batman drew closer and closer. Just as he braced himself for the full effect of the high-speed vehicle inches away, Batman swerved at the last second and slammed into a wall, unconscious.

The Joker's men had extricated themselves from the wreckage of the truck and were running to join their boss.

One of them knelt and grabbed at Batman's mask. There was the buzz of electricity. The man yelped, fell backward, and twitched. The Joker apparently thought that an associate taking maybe 50,000 volts was hilarious. He laughed, and was still laughing as he opened a switchblade and knelt next to Batman.

"Drop it," a familiar voice said.

"Just give me a second," said the Joker.

There was the sound of a pistol bullet being chambered and James Gordon said, "We got you, you son of a bitch."

Harvey Dent sat in the armored van waiting. The rear door swung open and he saw Jim Gordon.

"*Lieutenant*, you *do* like to play it pretty close to the chest."

"We got him, Harvey."

Dent nodded, and shook Gordon's hand.

Dent watched Gordon and the Joker leave in an unmarked car. He looked around for Batman, but he had already disappeared into the shadows. So much for thanking him, Dent thought . . . The ban on journalists had been lifted, and already the street was swarming with reporters and the tools of their trade. A dozen of them closed on Dent, brandishing microphones and cameras.

Ramirez shoved them back. "Let him be! He's been through enough."

"Thanks, Detective," Dent murmured. "I've got a date with a pretty upset fiancée."

"I figured, Counselor."

There was a ring of patrol cars around the Gotham Central lockup, and a pair of guards armed with riot guns at every entrance and at the tops and bottoms of every staircase.

The Joker sat alone in a holding cage. His makeup had run, his clothes were torn and soiled. Yet his erect posture and calm demeanor gave him an undeniable dignity. A uniformed officer struck the bars near the Joker's head with a nightstick; the Joker did not flinch.

James Gordon exploded. "Stand away, all of you. I don't want anything for his mob lawyer to use, understand? Handle this guy like he's made of glass."

The mayor entered the area and strode over to Gordon. They shook hands.

"Back from the dead?" the mayor boomed. "How'd you manage it, anyway?"

"Nothing fancy. Bulletproof vest. I let 'em think I was dead to help protect my family."

The mayor looked at the Joker. "What've we got?"

"Nothing," Gordon said. "No matches on prints, DNA, dental. Clothing is custom, no labels. Nothing in his pockets but knives and lint. No name, no other alias . . . nothing."

"Go home, Gordon. The clown'll keep till morning. Get some rest. You're going to need it. Tomorrow, you take the big job."

Gordon shook his head *no*.

"You don't have any say in the matter . . . *Commissioner* Gordon."

Gordon found that he had somehow misplaced his house keys and had to ring the front door bell. Barbara opened the door and stared at him slack-jawed, then slowly stepped aside. Gordon smiled and reached for her.

"You bastard," she said, and slapped him.

"I thought it was best if you didn't know—"

"Best for *who*? Me? Your kids? Or best for your *job*?"

Gordon started to apologize, but with a small cry Barbara was in his arms, her lips pressed against his in sheer happiness.

One of James Gordon's secrets was that every night he was home he read a bedtime story to his young son. He was just closing one of James, Junior's favorites, *The Stinky Cheese Man,* when the boy, who had seemed to be sleeping, spoke.

"Did Batman save you, Dad?"

Gordon stroked his son's hair. "Actually, this time I saved *him*."

Gordon's cell phone rang. He answered it as he was leaving his son's room, listened, then broke the connection. He went downstairs, kissed Barbara, promised her he'd be back as soon as possible, then left the house.

TWENTY-TWO

James Gordon pushed through a knot of detectives gathered in the observation room at Gotham Central and jerked a thumb at the Joker, visible both through a large glass window and on a video monitor.

"Has he said anything yet?" Gordon asked Ramirez.

Ramirez shook her head. Gordon moved past her and through a door. He sat at a table across from the Joker.

"Evening, Commissioner," the Joker said pleasantly.

"Harvey Dent never made it home," Gordon said.

"Of course not."

"What have you done with him?"

"Me? I was right here. Who did you leave him with? Your people? Assuming, of course, that they *are* your people and not Maroni's. Tell me . . . does it depress you to know how alone you are? Does it make you feel *responsible* for Harvey Dent's current predicament?"

"Where is he?"

"What time is it?"

"What difference does *that* make?"

"Depending on the time, he might be in one spot. Or several."

Somebody blabbed. One of the cops, or the courthouse people, or a civil servant—somebody trying to be nice, or seeking their fifteen minutes of fame, told a reporter that Dent had vanished, and within the hour the news was on all the local broadcasting venues and slated for the national network roundups.

Some of the print guys managed to squeeze it into late editions, others fretted that they'd have to wait another half day.

Alfred was dusting the library with the all-news radio station on as background company when he heard about Dent.

"Oh, dear Lord," he whispered.

Hours later, Gordon stood and unlocked the Joker's handcuffs. "If we're going to play games, I'm going to need a cup of coffee."

"The good-cop, bad-cop routine?"

Gordon was standing at the door, his hand on the knob. "Not exactly."

Gordon switched off the overhead light and left the

room. A few seconds later the light came back on, and Batman was standing behind the Joker.

Batman slammed the Joker's head on the table. When the Joker raised it, Batman was standing in front of him. The Joker wiped blood from his nose with the back of his wrist, and said, "Never start with the head. Victim gets fuzzy. Can't feel the next—"

Batman's fist smashed onto the Joker's fingers. The Joker's expression didn't change, and his voice remained pleasant. "See?"

"You wanted me. Here I am."

"I wanted to see what you'd *do*. And you didn't disappoint. You let five people die. Then you let Dent take your place. Even to a guy like me . . . that's *cold*."

"Where's Dent?"

"The mob fools want you dead so they can get back to the way things were," the Joker said, ignoring Batman's question. "But I know the truth—there *is* no going back. You've changed things. Forever."

"Then why do you want to kill me?"

The Joker laughed, then the laughing began to sound like sobbing.

"Kill you?" he gasped. "I don't want to kill you. What would I do without you? Go back to ripping off mob dealers? No, you . . ." He jabbed an index finger at Batman. "You. Complete. Me."

"You're garbage who kills for money."

"Don't talk like one of them. You're not, even if you'd like to be. To them, you're a freak like me. They just *need* you right now. But as soon as they don't, they'll cast you out like a leper."

The Joker half rose and stared into Batman's eyes. "Their morals, their code . . . It's a bad joke. Dropped at the first sign of trouble. They're only as good as the world *allows* them to be. You'll see. I'll show you. When the chips are down, these civilized people . . . they'll eat each other. See, I'm not a monster. I'm just ahead of the curve."

Batman grabbed the Joker's collar and hoisted him up. "Where's Dent."

"You have these rules, and you think they'll save you."

"I have *one* rule."

"Then that's the one you'll have to break. To know the truth."

"Which is?"

"The only sensible way to live in the world is without rules. Tonight, you're going to break your one rule . . ."

"I'm considering it."

"There are just moments left, so, you'll have to play my little game if you want to save . . . one of them."

"Them?"

"For a while I thought you really *were* Dent, the way you threw yourself after her—"

In the observation room, Gordon moved toward the door, realizing what was about to happen. But Batman had already jammed a chair under the doorknob. Then he picked up the Joker and threw him into the glass mirror. It splintered, and a single jagged shard fell to the floor. The Joker, bleeding from the nose and mouth, laughed.

"Look at you," he said to Batman in a chiding tone. "Does Harvey know about you and his . . ."

Batman flung the Joker across the table and into a wall.

"Killing is making a choice," the Joker said as though he were chatting with a dinner companion.

"*Where are they?*" Batman asked, and punched the Joker.

"You choose one life over the other," the Joker continued. "Your friend, the district attorney. Or his blushing bride to be."

Batman punched the Joker again . . .

. . . *and for a moment, less than a moment, remembered his dream, his father frowning, obviously angry, shouting words Bruce could not hear, but somehow understood anyway, words about means and ends and becoming what one beheld . . .*

The Joker spat out a tooth. "You have nothing. Nothing to threaten me with. Nothing to do with all your strength. But don't worry. I'm going to tell you where they are. Both of them. That's the point—you'll have to *choose*."

The Joker rubbed his hand over his chin, thoughtfully. The hand came away smeared with blood and makeup. "Let me see . . . Oh, yes. *He's* at 250 Fifty-second Boulevard. And *she's* at Avenue X at Cicero."

Batman went to the door, removed the chair, and entered the observation room.

"Which one are you going to?" Gordon asked.

Batman strode past him without slowing. "Dent knew the risks."

"He's going after Miss Dawes," Gordon said to his unit as he sprinted toward his car a few seconds later. "That makes Dent our job."

Rachel stayed in her office until she had heard, through official channels, that Harvey Dent was all right. On her way out of the courthouse, an officer whom she know from Gordon's squad asked her if she'd look at something odd. She followed the young woman into a corridor and—

Nothing. Then bumping. She was on the floor of a moving vehicle—a van?—and someone was telling her something she didn't understand, about her friends having to choose and only one making it . . .

And again nothing.

And she was sick to her stomach and her head was throbbing and . . . Where was she? Sitting in almost total darkness, the only light a thin, pale glow from some kind of crack and . . . she couldn't lift her hands, nor do more than wriggle her leg. Because she was bound? Yes.

Sitting, bound to a chair, in darkness, sick from whatever they used to knock her out, whoever *they* were.

"Can anyone hear me?" She tried to yell, but her voice was only a hoarse whisper.

But it was loud enough for Harvey Dent to hear. He had been awake for some minutes and could see, in the light from a single, bare and dirty bulb, that he was sitting tied to a rickety wooden chair in a filthy basement. Rachel's voice was coming from a speakerphone on the floor.

"Rachel? Rachel, is that you?"

"Harvey? Where are you?"

As soon as he had wakened, Dent had strained his head to look behind him. He knew that he was near two metal barrels, wired to a car battery and a crude timer that was counting down; its clock face showed five minutes. Five minutes to what? Nothing good.

It was now 4:35.

"It's okay, Rachel. Everything's going to be just fine."

The Joker was certainly damaged—bloody, smeared— but he seemed perfectly content, sitting in the interrogation room, guarded by Gerard Stephens.

"I want my phone call," he said.

"That's nice," Stephens said.

"How many of your friends have I killed?"

"I'm a twenty-year man. I can tell the difference between punks who need a little lesson in manners and the freaks like you who would just enjoy it. So I'm not gonna hit you. And you killed six of my friends."

"You know why I use a knife, Detective? Guns are too quick. You don't get to savor all the little emotions. See, in their last moments, people show you who they really are. So, in a way, I knew your friends better than you ever did. Would you like to know which of them were really cowards?"

The night shift was busy in the holding area adjoining the lockup, uniforms and detectives alike processing the Joker's crew: taking fingerprints, photographing, asking simple questions. A badly overweight man who had identified himself as Kilson was pleading for a doctor.

"I don't feel so good," he moaned, clutching his belly.

"You're a cop killer," a detective named Murphy said. "You're lucky to be feeling anything below the neck."

"We better get a medic," a sergeant said, turning to a uniformed officer standing next to him. "Remember what Gordon told us . . . everything by the book."

"I think some of the ambulance guys are still outside," said the cop. "I'll see if any of 'em feel like getting their hands dirty."

As Rachel's eyes had adjusted to the dark, she began to discern silhouettes and, comparing her situation with the one Harvey Dent described to her, she realized that they were in identical predicaments: helpless and close to ticking bombs. She began to realize, for the first time, that she might not survive, or that Harvey might not, and she was filled with regret for all she had not said to him, for her reservations about loving him. Should she speak now?

"Can you move your chair?" Dent asked her.

"No." Rachel could see the red numbers on the timer. "Harvey, we don't have much time."

2:47

2:46

2:45

Her confession to Harvey would have to wait. Because she had to believe that, somehow, they would both come through this ordeal intact. Right now, she had to concentrate on escape.

1:56

Dent could move his chair by tilting his weight until it was mostly on a rear leg, pivoting on that leg, and repeating the process on the other side. That's what he was doing, inching closer to the barrels and sweating and talking to Rachel: "Look for something to free yourself."

"They said only one of us was going to make it," Rachel said. "That they'd let our . . . our friends choose."

Dent's chair wouldn't move—stuck on a raised board, probably. Dent shifted all his weight to one side and . . . that was a mistake. He began to topple. It was too late to regain his balance, and he fell into one of the barrels, knocking it over, falling on top of it and slipping to the floor. The concrete was cold against his cheek, then it was cold and wet; the top of the barrel had dropped open, and diesel fuel was spilling out.

1:23

"Harvey," Rachel called. "What's happening?"

"Nothing. I'm trying to—" Dent gagged: Some of the fuel had touched his lips, filling his mouth and nose with an ugly taste and an overpowering stink.

Fuel continued to seep out onto the floor and onto Dent, soaking through his clothing, wetting his skin, making it itch and sting, the fumes rising into his nostrils and mouth and eyes. He had never, never felt so uncomfortable, so helpless and trapped, and if he had been in this situation alone, he might have simply surrendered to it. But he had to save himself and in so doing, find a way to save Rachel.

59 seconds

Rachel knew, now, that they wouldn't escape, that one or both of them would be dead in less than a minute. But there was still time. She could still tell Harvey what she felt.

34 seconds

"Harvey, in case . . . I want you to know something . . ."

"Don't think like that, Rachel."

"I know, but I don't *want* them to . . ."

20

19

18

"I don't want to live without you, Harvey. Because I do have an answer, and my answer is *yes* . . ."

Murphy escorted an ambulance paramedic to where Kilson sat handcuffed to a bench.

"Where's it hurt?" the medic asked.

Kilson pointed to his belly.

"Let's get your shirt off," the medic said.

Gerry Stephens stepped from the interrogation room with the Joker holding a piece of broken glass to his throat. A half dozen detectives stopped what they were doing and stared. Two of them reached for holstered pistols.

"This is my own damn fault," Stephens said. "Just shoot him."

"What do you want?" Murphy asked the Joker.

"I *want*," the Joker said slowly, as though speaking to a toddler, "my phone call. Please."

Murphy looked around at the other detectives, shrugged, took a cell phone from his hip pocket, and tossed it to the Joker, who managed to catch it in his left hand while keeping the shard in his right pressed against Stephens's throat. The Joker began to press keys with his thumb.

The medic stared down at the rectangular shape under Kilson's skin, which bore a line of crude stitches. It was about the size and shape of a playing card, and a bit thicker.

"Is that a . . . phone?" the medic muttered. "Somebody stuck a phone in this guy."

The detectives looked at each other, their expressions saying: *Well, this is a new one . . .* Murphy took a step backward, but craned his head forward to maintain his view of Kilson.

The Joker pressed the SEND button on Murphy's phone, and Kilson's belly . . . started ringing. The medic and several officers leaned in closer in disbelief. Three seconds later, an explosion tore through the room.

Batman encountered little traffic once he got past central Gotham and into the area of warehouses and manufacturing lofts that formed a half-mile barrier between the city and the first of the suburbs. It wasn't a region people ever went to except on business, and at this hour everyone had gone home. He braked the pod at the corner of Avenue X and Cicero Street and before the engine had died he was kicking in the door to a storage facility. He saw that he was in some kind of shipping depot: cardboard boxes were stacked at irregular intervals, and there were a couple of forklifts parked against a wall. There was a glimmer of light coming from a flight of steps that ran downward, obviously to a basement. Batman ran, down the stairs, then through another door.

He had expected to see Rachel, to free her and get her out of the building. To tell her he loved her and would keep her safe forever. Instead, he saw Harvey Dent lying in a black puddle, bound to a chair. Next to him were two barrels, one on its side, and a timer. Shock and horror flooded over Batman.

"No!" Dent rasped. "Not me! Why did you come for *me*?"

Rachel, thought Batman. *Good God, I've failed her . . .*

9

8

7

Cursing and furious with himself, Batman dragged Dent and the chair toward the door, desperately trying to free the sobbing, struggling man.

"*RACHEL!*" Dent screamed.

The Joker stopped outside Lau's cell and beckoned to him with a forefinger. "Time to take a little ride."

Strapped to her chair, hearing Harvey's screams, Rachel realized she was going to die. No one was going to save her. Tears ran down her cheeks as she tried to accept that this was how her life was going to end. "Bruce," she said. "Harvey . . . I love you."

4

3

2

Gordon's car had just stopped at 250 Second Avenue, an abandoned warehouse in the middle of the block, when an explosion shattered windows—

Batman wrapped his cape around Dent and lifted him along with the chair, then hurled him through the door. A deafening noise and a sphere of flame filled the room and enveloped the two men.

———

Gordon was running toward the storefront that was gouting fire from every window. A patrolman brought him down with a tackle, and several others helped restrain him.

"There's nothin' you can do," the officer gasped.

Dent's fuel-soaked clothing was burning. Batman smothered the flames with his cape and smashed the chair, and once Dent was free, he began to carry Dent through the conflagration toward the steps. Dent's clothes caught fire again, but this time Batman was on the staircase, and it was collapsing under him. Batman got them both to the street outside and rolled Dent over and over until the fire was out.

Gordon and the uniforms stood watching firemen contain the blaze. They weren't trying to save the warehouse—clearly, that was impossible. But they could save the adjoining buildings.

Gordon noticed hundreds of playing cards blowing across the asphalt. He picked one up and, in the orange glow of the fire, saw that it was a playing card, a joker, with Lau's face atop the clown's shoulders.

A sergeant Gordon didn't know approached, and said, "Dent's alive."

Gordon looked at the fire. "How?"

"The Joker must've lied. Dent was at the other place, on Avenue X."

Still gazing at the fire, Gordon said, "Then Rachel Dawes . . ."

"Can't be sure till we can get in there. Maybe mid-morning. But yeah, the bet would be that Miss Dawes is inside that. Oh, yeah, another thing. The Joker's gone. Something blew up in MCU. Lau's gone, too."

"*Goddammit!!!* The Joker *planned* to be caught. He *wanted* me to lock him up in the MCU. That son of a bitch!" Gordon tore at his hair and broke down in sobs.

TWENTY-THREE

Batman had arrived a few minutes after Gordon and his men started mopping up and putting out the fire. He approached the burning building and stood silent for several long minutes, trying to suppress the urge to scream and start tearing things apart. As he turned to leave, he noticed the glimmer of metal in the glare of the fire's flames. He bent down and picked the object up, realizing that it was Harvey's coin. He must have given it to Rachel at some point. He put it in a pouch on his utility belt.

Rachel . . .

Alfred Pennyworth was feeling horrible grief for the first time since Thomas and Martha Wayne had died. He'd gotten a hasty call from Master Bruce, and he knew what had happened. Now, Alfred sat at the kitchen table reading the letter Rachel had written to Bruce and had given to him for safekeeping.

Dear Bruce,

I need to explain, and I need to be honest and clear. I'm going to marry Harvey Dent. I love him and want to spend the rest of my life with him. When I told you that if Gotham no longer needed a Batman we could be together, I meant it. But I'm not sure the day will come when you no longer need Batman, and if it does, I will be there, but as your friend. I'm sorry to let you down. If you lose your faith in me, please keep our faith in people.

Love, now and always,
Rachel

Alfred wiped tears from his eyes, refolded the letter, put it back in its envelope, and placed it on a breakfast tray he brought into the bedroom. Bruce, still wearing his Batman outfit, the cowl on the floor by his feet, was slumped in a chair staring out the window at the Gotham skyline.

"I prepared a little breakfast," Alfred said.

"Okay. Alfred?"

"Yes, Master Bruce?"

"Did I bring this on us? On her? I thought I would inspire good, not madness."

"You *have* inspired good. But you spat in the face of

Gotham's criminals—didn't you think there might be casualties? Things were always going to have to get worse before they got better."

"But *Rachel* . . . Alfred, I *loved* her. A part of me still thought we'd have a life together. That when this was all over we'd . . ." Bruce broke off, unable to finish the sentence. He swiped tears from his eyes as Alfred laid a hand on his shoulder.

"Rachel believed in what you stand for. What *we* stand for. Gotham needs you."

"Gotham needs its hero. And I let the Joker blow him half to hell."

"Which is why, for now, they'll have to make do with *you*."

Bruce finally turned his head and looked up at Alfred. "She was going to wait for me. Dent doesn't know. He can *never* know."

Bruce looked at the tray and saw the envelope. "What's that?"

Putting the envelope in his pocket, Alfred said, "It can wait." He turned to leave.

"Alfred? The story you were telling me, the bandit in the forest, in Burma . . . Did you catch him?"

Alfred nodded.

"How?'

Alfred waited almost a minute before answering, "We burned the forest down."

He turned and left, and Bruce was again alone in his thoughts.

Alfred reentered the bedroom less than a minute later and switched on the television. To Bruce, who was still sitting staring out the window, he said, "You need to see this."

Bruce swiveled in his chair and looked at the familiar face of Mike Engel, the TV reporter, who was saying, ". . . he's a credible source, an A and M lawyer for a prestigious consultancy. He says he's waited as long as he can for Batman to do the right thing. Now he's taking matters into his own hands. We'll be live at five with the true identity of the Batman. Stay with us."

Harvey Dent knew his face was burned badly and that he couldn't eat normally. He could speak, though, from one side of his mouth; the words were slurred, but audible and understandable. He watched James Gordon enter the room and sit at his bedside.

"I'm sorry about Rachel," Gordon said. Dent did not reply, and any change in his expression was hidden by the bandages. Gordon spoke again: "The doctor says you're in agonizing pain but won't accept medication. That you're refusing skin grafts."

"Remember the name you all had for me when I was at Internal Affairs?" Dent asked. "What was it?"

"Harvey, I can't . . ."

"*Say it!*"

"Two-face," Gordon whispered. "Harvey Two-face."

Dent turned his head toward Gordon and revealed what the flames had done to him. The left side of his face had become a horror: skin blackened and shriveled, molars visible through a gash in his cheek, the eye reduced to a ball and socket.

Gordon did not look away.

Dent smiled with the right side of his mouth. "Why should I hide who I am?"

"I know you tried to warm me," Gordon said. "I'm sorry. Wuertz was driving you home. Was he working for them? Do you know who picked up Rachel? Harvey, I need to know which of my men I can trust."

"Why would you listen to me *now*?"

"I'm sorry, Harvey."

"No you're not. Not yet."

Gordon sat silently for a while, then got up and left. It was then that Harvey noticed something on a side table. Something metallic and glinting in the lamp-light . . .

Maroni, on crutches, clumped down the corridor. "H'lo, Lieutenant—or it is *Commissioner* now?"

"What happened to you, Sal?"

"I fell off a fire escape. But never mind that. What I wanna talk about is this craziness—it's too much."

"You should have thought of that before you let the clown out of the box."

"You want him, I can tell you where he'll be this afternoon."

The sun was low in the sky when the black SUV left the freeway via its last exit in lower Gotham and went through narrow, cobblestoned streets until it reached the tip of the city, an area as yet untouched by urban renewal, a dense warren of abandoned buildings and stores and wharves too rotted to use. The SUV bumped onto one of these and braked next to an ancient freighter, listing and sheeted with rust. The Chechen got out of the SUV and, followed by dogs and bodyguards, went up a wobbly gangway and onto the ship. He climbed into a hatch and descended a ladder into a cavernous hold. There were a dozen battery-powered lanterns placed at intervals around the bulkheads, their beams aimed at a pile of cash in the center of the chamber. The Joker was perched atop the pile. Lau, bound, was lying at the bottom. Several bulky men were standing in the shadows.

The Chechen spoke, his words echoing off the steel walls. "You bring friends."

"I gave each one of them a nice handful of your cash," the Joker said. "I'm sure you don't mind. Loyalty *can* be bought."

"Like I say, you not so crazy as you look."

The Joker slid down the pile of money. "I'm a man of my word." The Joker put a flat hand over his eyes and gazed around. "But where's the Italian?"

The Chechen, in the process of lighting a cigar, shrugged. "More for us," he said, blue smoke seeping from his mouth. "What you do with all your money, Joker?"

The Joker danced around to the rear of the pile and emerged from the other side holding a gasoline can. "I'm a man of simple tastes. I like gunpowder. Dynamite." He splashed liquid from the can onto the money. "*Gasoline.*"

The Chechen bolted forward and stopped when the Joker jammed a pistol into his cheek.

"You know what they have in common?" the Joker continued. "They're *cheap.*"

"You said you were a man of your word."

The Joker plucked the cigar from between the Chechen's lips. "I am."

He tossed the smoldering cigar onto the money pile.

The Chechen stared in horror as the money flared into flame.

"I'm only burning my half," the Joker said. "Of course, *your* half will burn with it. Nothing to be done, I'm afraid."

The Chechen watched the fire.

"All you care about is the money," the Joker said. "This city deserves a better class of criminal, and I'm going to give it to them. This is *my* town now. Tell your men they work for *me.*"

"They won't work for a freak."

The Joker removed a knife from a sheath under his jacket and tossed it to one of his men. "Cut him up and offer him to his little princes. Let's show him just how loyal a hungry dog is."

Two other men grabbed the Chechen.

The fire had burned down, almost to where Lau was lying.

"It's not about the money," the Joker said. "It's about sending a message."

Lau screamed as the Joker took a cell phone from his pocket.

At that moment, a lot of Gotham residents were watching television—not so much the usual afternoon talk show/cartoon rerun fare, but the all-news channel, where Mike Engel was interviewing Coleman Reese. Even less media-savvy Gothamites could tell that Engel was milking the story for all it was worth, delaying Reese's big revelation by taking calls.

". . . how much they gonna pay you to say who the Batman really is," an irate viewer was asking Reese.

"That's simply not why I'm doing this," Reese said, looking straight into the camera.

"Caller, you're on the air," Engel said to nobody visible.

The caller, a man with a deep voice: "Harvey Dent didn't want us to give in to this maniac. You think you know better than him?"

"Guy's got a point," Engel said, as earnest as a school debater's referee. "Dent didn't want Batman to give himself up. Is this the right thing to do?"

Just as earnestly, Reese said, "If Dent could talk now, he might feel differently."

"And we wish him a speedy recovery," Engel said, now a model of sincerity. "God knows we need him now. Let's take another call."

The disembodied voice, a falsetto, seemed to be that of an old lady. "Mr. Reese, what's more valuable, one life or a hundred?"

"I guess it would depend on the life," Reese replied, a small smile on his lips.

"Okay, let's say it's your life. Is it worth more than the lives of several hundred others?"

"Of course not," Reese said, now apparently indignant.

"I'm glad you feel that way. Because I've put a bomb in one of the city's hospitals. It's going off in sixty minutes unless someone kills you."

"Who is this?" Engel demanded.

"Just a concerned citizen"—the falsetto vanished, the voice dropped an octave—"and regular guy. I had a vision. Of a world without Batman. The mob ground out a little profit and the police tried to shut them down, one block at a time . . . and it was so . . . boring. I've had a change of heart. I don't want Mr. Reese spoiling everything, but why should *I* have all the fun? Let's give someone else a chance . . ."

Reese rose from his chair. Engel put a hand on his shoulder and pushed him back down.

"If Coleman Reese isn't dead in sixty minutes, then I blow up a hospital. Of course, you could always kill yourself, Mr. Reese. But that would be a noble thing to do. And you're a lawyer."

There was a loud *click* and the hum of a dial tone.

The cops at the Major Crimes Unit had been taking turns watching television, just in case the Joker chose to make another announcement, and they weren't disappointed. Detective Murphy was on monitor duty, snacking from a bag of corn chips, when the pseudo old lady began her rant. He realized immediately what was happening and yelled to the rest of the squad, including Gordon and a dozen uniforms, to join him. Gordon quickly addressed the patrolmen.

"Call in every officer—tell 'em to head to the nearest hospital and start evac and search. Call the transit authority, the school board, prisons. Get every available bus to a hospital. Murphy, you're in charge of that. The priority is Gotham General—wheel everybody out of that place right now. My hunch is, that's where the bomb is."

"Why?" a sergeant asked.

"That's where Harvey Dent is."

The uniforms hurried away, and Gordon turned to his detectives.

"You guys come with me."

"Where we going?" one of them asked.

"To get Reese."

As Alfred switched off the television, Bruce Wayne was already moving toward the elevator. Alfred caught up with him seconds later.

"Get to the comm gear," Bruce said. "I need you plugged in, checking Gordon's men and their families."

"Looking for?"

"Hospital admissions."

"Will you be taking the Bat-Pod, sir?"

Gordon and his men burst into the television station, running through the reception area and onto the broadcast studio without asking permission or even flashing their badges. They found Reese slumped in a chair just beyond the glare of the lights and grabbed him.

Mike Engel bolted from his on-camera desk, and asked Gordon, "Do you really think someone would try to . . ."

Gordon ignored him and hustled Reese into the lobby. Through the glass doors, Gordon saw an old man raise a big revolver and begin pulling the trigger. The door shattered as Gordon flung Reese to the carpet.

Gordon did not fire back. He pulled Reese back into the studio and told Murphy to get the cars to the rear of the building.

Gordon and his men surrounded Reese during the dozen steps they took from the back door of the studio to a waiting police van.

"They're trying to kill me," Reese gasped.

Gordon pushed Reese into the back of the van. "Maybe the Batman'll save you."

Bruce was certain that he knew what Gordon would do, and he was right: get Reese to safety and everyone out of the hospitals. Nothing he could do about the hospital inmates, though their well-being should obviously have the highest priority; his appearance might only confuse an already chaotic situation. But Reese . . . maybe he could help there.

He guided the Lamborghini off the freeway and toward the television station. When he saw the mob in the street, he thought that Gordon would probably leave by the alley, and when he saw the police van pulling away from behind the station, he knew he'd made a good guess. He began to follow.

Detectives Jeremy Polk and Willy Davis were on the four-to-midnight shift outside Harvey Dent's room at Gotham General when the word came to get everyone out, and that meant Harvey Dent as well, ASAP. Polk and Davis checked the room, then Polk left Davis standing by Dent's bed while he went to the street outside to see what he could scare up in the way of transportation. He found a school bus at the emergency-room entrance, its engine idling; orderlies, doctors, and nurses were helping men and women dressed in white hospital gowns and robes to board it.

Polk saw the driver standing near the open front door.

"I got a priority passenger," Polk said.

"We'll make a spot for 'im," the driver said.

Polk keyed his radio: "Davis, I got space, bring him out."

No answer.

"Davis?"

Polk ran back into the hospital and up the fire stairs to Dent's room. There was no sign of Davis. A red-haired nurse stood over Dent's bed with her back to Polk.

"Ma'am, we're going to have to move him now," Polk said, and got no answer. "Ma'am?"

The nurse turned and fired a silenced pistol. Polk died as he fell to the floor.

Then the nurse pulled off her cap, and said to Dent, "It's me, your old pal the Joker. Surprised? I don't want there to be any hard feelings between us, Harvey. When you and Rachel were being abducted, I was sitting in Gordon's cage. I didn't rig those charges."

"Your men," Dent croaked. "Your plan."

"Do I really look like a man with a plan, Harvey? *I* don't have a plan. The mob has plans, the cops have plans. You know what I am, Harvey? I'm a dog chasing cars. I wouldn't know what to do with one if I caught it. I just *do* things. I'm a wrench in the gears. I *hate* plans. Yours, theirs, everyone's. Maroni has plans. Gordon has plans. Schemers trying to control their worlds. I'm not a schemer. I show schemers how pathetic their attempts to control things really are. So when I say that what happened to you and your girlfriend was nothing personal, you know *I'm* telling the truth."

The Joker gave Dent his pistol and stood still as Dent aimed it. The Joker leaned forward, pressing his head against the gun barrel. "It's the schemer who put you where you are. You were a schemer. You had plans. Look where it got you. I just did what I did best—I took your plan and I turned it on itself. Look what I've done to this city with a few drums of gas and a couple of bullets. Nobody panics when the *expected* people get killed. Nobody panics when things go according to plan, even if the plan is horrifying. If I tell the press that tomorrow a gangbanger will get shot, or a truckload of soldiers will be blown up, nobody panics. Because it's all part of the plan. But when I say that one little old mayor will die, everybody loses their minds! Introduce a little anarchy, you upset the established order, and everything becomes chaos. I'm an agent of chaos. And you know the thing about chaos, Harvey? It's *fair*."

Dent was holding his lucky coin. He had found it on his bedside table after he had spoken to Gordon in the hospital. He was not sure how it had gotten there, as the last he remembered, he had given the coin to Rachel. It was burned and dirty on one side due to the fire. Just like he was now . . . He looked down at it: good side.

"You live," he said.

He turned the coin over: bad side.

"You die."

The Joker looked first at the coin, then, admiringly, at Dent. "*Now* you're talking!"

Dent flipped the coin, caught it, then looked at it.

Gordon sat with Reese and a cop named Berg in the back of the van. He still didn't know where he wanted to take the lawyer, but he knew plenty of places he *didn't* want Reese to be, and for now, his agenda was to get away from all of them.

He looked at his companion. "I don't think we've officially met. Berg, isn't it?"

"Yes, sir, Commissioner Gordon," Berg said, looking at his watch.

"Something's eating at you, son. Maybe I'd better have your weapon."

"My wife's in the hospital, Commissioner. She's very sick. I don't want her to be in any more danger—"

Berg stopped midsentence and took out his gun, but he didn't give it to Gordon. Instead, he aimed it at Gordon's head. "He said he'd kill my wife. I'm sorry, sir."

_____

Bruce, a half block behind the van, saw it stop at a red light. The light changed, the van inched into the intersection. A battered green pickup truck shot from out of a side street, aimed toward the police van. Bruce gripped the wheel of the Lamborghini and floored the gas pedal, twisted the steering wheel, jumped the curb, and sped down the sidewalk.

The pickup was only feet from the van, about to hit it broadside.

The Lamborghini slid between the pickup and the van, and the pickup smashed into it.

Inside the van, the jolt knocked Berg against the wall. Gordon's own gun was already out and slamming the side of Berg's head before the younger man could recover.

Gordon handcuffed the unconscious Berg, told Reese to stay put, and climbed onto the street. He went to the fancy sports car, wrenched open the door, and reached inside to help the driver.

Then he saw who the man was, and whispered, "Bruce Wayne?"

Bruce got out of the Lamborghini, now a mass of twisted metal, and swayed. Gordon put a hand on his arm to steady him and guided him to the curb. Bruce sat, put his head in his hands for a moment, then looked up at Gordon.

"You okay, Mr. Wayne?"

"Call me Bruce. I think so."

"That was a brave thing you did."

"Trying to catch the light?"

"You weren't protecting the van?"

"Why? Who's in it?"

"You don't watch a whole lot of news, do you, Mr. Wayne?"

Bruce shrugged. "It can get a little depressing. Do you think I should go to a hospital?"

"Not today."

The Joker sauntered through the deserted hospital, his right thumb on the button of a detonator. He pressed it and, as he continued walking, explosions burst from the doors behind him. He went through an exit, and windows blew out, sending showers of glass into the rays of the dying sun.

The evacuees, those who could walk, sought cover behind the bus or simply by flattening themselves onto the asphalt.

The Joker walked into the emergency-room area and onto the school bus as Gotham General imploded and collapsed, filling the air with dust and smoke and debris.

Gordon heard the sounds, a series of loud bangs followed by a prolonged rumble, and saw, over the tops of buildings, dust and smoke rising into the twilight.

"Gotta be Gotham General," he said, keying his radio.

A cop named Grogan responded. Gordon asked him if Dent had been evacuated, and Grogan replied that he thought so, but wasn't sure.

Everyone in the area was staring at what had been Gotham General just two minutes earlier and was now a huge heap of twisted steel and shattered masonry from which dust and smoke still rose. No one paid any particular attention to the school bus that left the space that had been a parking zone for the emergency room and, bumping over stuff that littered the pavement, turned onto the nearest street.

By six, every television and radio venue in the city had preempted regular programming and was covering the Gotham General situation. But the reporters had no new information, so they continually repeated video of the hospital collapsing taken by a passerby with a phone camera, interviewed each other, interviewed eyewitnesses, who all said the same thing: it had been blown up.

But the journalists soldiered on, and people continued to wonder and worry and talk. Some thought that this latest hassle, coming so soon after the Narrows drama the other year, was the universe telling them that *anywhere* would be better than Gotham City, maybe including the Black Hole of Calcutta. One small but noisy group thought that the Joker was part of a government plot designed to distract the citizenry from their loss of independence—a couple of radio-talk-show hosts rode that theory to exhaustion. The *Gotham Times* began to print a lot of angry letters, mostly expressing chagrin at the cops' inability to do their job, which was to serve and protect—especially protect. Most people, though, did what Gothamites almost always do: complain, hope that the evil, whatever it was, stayed clear of *their* neighborhood, and took out the garbage and grumbled to their mates and . . . lived their lives. But there were a lot of small changes in their routines. More parents drove their kids to school and soccer practice and the skating rink, and forbade them to hang out at the malls. Business was sharply down at downtown restaurants and theaters. Gasoline sales were also suffering because people weren't going anywhere they didn't absolutely have to be. The only thing that was improving were the ratings for the nightly newscasts. The good citizens of Gotham City were watching a lot of news.

They were watching in Lou's Bar, a drinking establishment on the fringe of the blue-collar neighborhood where Detective Michael Wuertz lived alone in a three-room flat. Lou's was not a classy joint. It was dingy and stale-smelling, with bad lighting and worse plumbing, where a despairing and lonely man could go to extinguish large chunks of time. After dinner was usually the big time of day for Lou's, when it became a haven for guys who couldn't stand the thought of either another evening of TV or another argument with their wives. Now, at six fifteen, only Wuertz and the bartender were in Lou's, and only the bartender was watching the news broadcast on a television set on metal brackets above the back bar.

"Sweet Jesus, d'you see this, Mike?" he asked Wuertz. "They blew up a hospital. Shouldn't you be out there, y'know, doing something?"

"It's my day off," Wuertz mumbled into his drink.

The bartender locked the cash register and came around the bar. "I gotta take a leak. Keep an eye on things, will ya?"

Wuertz shrugged an answer. The bartender went through a door. Almost immediately, the door reopened.

"What?" Wuertz grumbled. "You need me to shake it for y—"

Someone jammed a gun barrel into Wuertz's cheek. He looked sideways, without turning his head, and recognized the gunman standing in deep shadow, with only the right side of his face visible.

"Hello," Harvey Dent said. "I see you still come to the same old place."

"Dent! I thought you was . . . dead."

Dent leaned into the light, displaying the mutilated left side of his face. "Half."

Dent picked up Wuertz's drink, took a sip, asked, "Who picked up Rachel, Wuertz?"

"It must've been Maroni's men."

Dent slammed the glass onto the bar. "You, of all people, are gonna protect the other traitor in Gordon's unit?"

"I don't know who it is. He'd never tell *me*."

Neither man spoke for a full minute. Finally, Wuertz said, "I swear to God I didn't know what they were gonna do to you."

Dent took his lucky coin from his pocked. "Funny, I don't know what's gonna happen to you, either."

Dent flipped the coin, caught it, looked at the damaged side, then pulled the trigger.

Jim Gordon had a bad night. He crawled into bed a bit after one, lay still, rolled over, got up and had a glass of milk, retired again and watched the windowpane lighten. It was 5:00 A.M. Good time to go to work as any. He scribbled a note to Barbara, propped it against the toaster, and drove through semideserted streets to the grotesque heap that had been a hospital.

There were already dozens of men and women busy at the disaster site, most of them wearing hard hats. He saw one of the cops, Grogan, talking to a paramedic. He asked Grogan for a situation report, and Grogan said there *was* no situation report.

"You must know how many were inside," Gordon protested. "You've got patient lists, roll calls . . ."

Grogan interrupted him. "Sir. Sir. Take a look at what we're dealing with. Cops, National Guard, sanitation men, firemen . . . As near as we can figure, we've got fifty missing. But that building was *clear*. I checked it myself, and so did six other cops." He waved toward a departing bus. "These vehicles are heading off to other hospitals. My guess is, we missed one."

"Yeah? What's your guess about where Harvey Dent is?"

Grogan said nothing.

"Keep looking," Gordon said. "And keep it to yourself."

TWENTY-FOUR

Lucius Fox expected to find Bruce Wayne in the research and development facility, in a subsubbasement of the Wayne Enterprises building. Instead, he found an array of thousands of tiny monitors. As he approached, seemingly random patterns appeared on them, patterns that swirled and dissolved and gradually re-formed themselves into a map.

Batman spoke from the shadows. "Beautiful, isn't it?"

"Beautiful," Fox said. "Unethical. *Dangerous.* You've turned every phone in the city into a microphone."

"And a high-frequency generator-receiver."

"Like the phone I gave you in Hong Kong. You took my sonar concept and applied it to every phone in he city. With half the city feeding you sonar, you can image all of Gotham. This is *wrong*!"

"I've got to find this man, Lucius."

"But at what cost?"

"The database is null-key encrypted. It can only be accessed by one person."

"No one should have that kind of power."

"That's why I gave it to you."

"Spying on 30 million people wasn't in my job description."

"Let me show you something I recorded from a newscast." Batman turned on a full-size monitor.

The Joker appeared on the screen. "What does it take to make you people want to join in? You failed to kill the lawyer. I've got to get you off the bench and into the game. So, here it is . . . Come nightfall, the city is mine, and anyone left here plays by my rules. If you don't want to be in the game, get out now. But the bridge-and-tunnel crowd are in for a surprise."

Batman switched off the monitor, and said to Fox, "Trust me." He plugged a USB dongle into the console. "This is the audio sample. If he talks within range of any phone in the city, you'll be able to triangulate his position. When you've finished, type in your name to turn it off."

"This is a terrible weight you've put on me. I didn't ask for it, I don't want it. I'll help you this one time . . . but as long as this machine is at Wayne Enterprises, I won't be."

Then began the great exodus. At first hundreds of thousands, and at the end, millions of men, women, and children streamed past the city limits—on foot, by car and motorcycle and bicycle, and a few by boat. Many did not reach their destinations, whatever they were; there were overheated engines and blown tires and, mostly, empty fuel tanks because few anticipated being stranded in traffic jams for hours. There were heart attacks and panic attacks and asthma attacks. There were fistfights and a few gunfights among motorists driven past fury by frustration. Some acts of kindness occurred, but those grew rarer as the day wore on.

State police did what they could. It wasn't much.

The sky over everyone's head buzzed with small aircraft, mostly television helicopters. Like their studio-bound colleagues, the airborne reporters didn't have much to report on but, like their studio-bound colleagues, this did not prevent them from talking into microphones. The information they conveyed could be easily summarized: It sure is a mess.

Of course, not everyone fled the city. Most Gothamites stayed put and braced themselves for some inconvenience, some belt-tightening, maybe a little pain. *What the hell, it's Gotham . . . what can you expect? Lousy town . . .*

Lucius Fox considered his options. He could just pull a Pontius Pilate, wash his hands of the whole thing, good-bye Mr. Wayne, and good luck. But he wouldn't. He had never once, in his sixty years, broken a promise, and he'd promised Wayne he'd stay on until the present crisis was past. Okay, maybe promise-keeping was really nothing more than a habit, but it had helped give him the parts of himself that he liked. He would, though what Wayne had done with the technology Lucius had given him was, in Lucius's opinion, pure evil. He had no doubt that Bruce Wayne was a good man, but he was starting to doubt Bruce's nocturnal alter ego, and the lengths he seemed willing to go to. The lines that had been crossed . . . Maybe this was one of those three-faces-of-Eve deals, different personalities inhabiting the same body. And maybe Lucius wasn't serving the *good* personality anymore.

How the hell to know? Batman was trying to put the skids under a rotten bastard, no doubt about that, maybe save some lives, but he was abusing everything Lucius held sacred to do it.

He made his decision. He'd keep his promise, but he wouldn't just walk away. He would destroy every trace of the technology, beginning with the hardware already operating. Then he'd get rid of the computer files and finish up by burning every scrap of paper in the lab. If Bruce Wayne betrayed him, tried to use the technology again, or, worse, give it to someone else, someone governmental maybe, he'd have a hard time, he's have to start—well, maybe not from scratch, because once you knew that something had already been done you had a big head start on doing it yourself. But Lucius's sabotage would slow Bruce down, a lot.

Lucius hated this, hated every damn bit of it. Because next to keeping promises, being grateful when gratitude was due was his primary virtue, and he had plenty to thank Bruce Wayne for.

You take the hand you're dealt, you play it, you don't whine.

Gordon was doing his best. This wasn't the kind of thing he had any experience with, nor any training, but that didn't stop him from trying. At the moment, he was in City Hall, in the mayor's office, reporting to his honor.

"My officers are going over every inch of the tunnels and bridges," Gordon was saying, "but with the Joker's threat . . ."

"Land routes east?" the mayor asked.

"Backed up for hours. Which leaves the ferries with thirty thousand waiting to board. Plus, corrections are at capacity, so I want to use the ferry to take some prisoners off the island."

"The men you and Dent put away? Those aren't people I'm worried about."

"You *should* be. They're the people you least want to be stuck with in an emergency. Whatever the Joker's planning, it's a good bet that Harvey's prisoners might be involved. I want 'em out of here."

Gordon prevailed. An hour later, officers in riot gear

escorted citizens off one of the ferries and felons on. Nobody was happy.

Sal Maroni climbed into the rear of the limo and settled his bulk into the leather seat. He was in a hurry. Wanted to meet the old lady before dark.

"Hey driver," he said, louder than was necessary. "Don't stop for lights, cops, nothing."

"Going to join your wife?" a familiar voice asked. The man beside the driver leaned over the seat, aiming a pistol, letting the light from outside the car strike his mutilated face.

"Do you love her?" Dent continued, ignoring Maroni's gasp.

"Yes."

"Can you imagine what it would be like to listen to her die?"

"Take it up with the Joker. He killed your woman. Made you like this."

"The Joker's just a mad dog. I want whoever let him off his leash. I took care of Wuertz, but who was your other man inside Gordon's unit? Who picked up Rachel? It must've been someone she trusted."

"If I tell you, willl you let me go?"

"It can't hurt your chances."

"It was Ramirez."

Dent took his lucky coin from his pocket and cocked his pistol.

"But you said—" Maroni protested.

"I said it couldn't hurt your chances."

Dent flipped the coin, caught it: good side. "Lucky guy."

Dent flipped the coin again: bad side. "But *he's* not."

"Who?" Maroni asked, confused.

The limo made its way out of the train yard.

Dent fastened his seat belt and shot the driver.

The limo sped forward and crashed into an abandoned shack, then flipped over, crashed beyond repair.

TWENTY-FIVE

The first ferry was chugging away from its dock and into the bay as the moon became visible through clouds, a fuzzy white disc. As soon as the traffic cops signaled the deckhands to lift the boarding barrier on the second ferry, hundreds of people surged aboard, some burdened with luggage, some wearing fur coats, some dressed as though for a beach outing, despite the chilly air. Within minutes, it, too, pulled out into the choppy water, heading for the western shore, the mainland, safety.

It was about a half mile from the city when, Kirk Packer, the first mate of the vessel carrying the prisoners, went on deck and did something he always liked to do when he was working at night, gaze at the lights of Gotham. From out here, in the semidarkness, Gotham was beautiful. He noticed that the sister vessel, the second ferry, the one full of citizens, was a motionless silhouette, dead in the water.

He went onto the bridge and said to the captain, "They've lost their engines . . . the other guys. Get on the radio and tell 'em we'll come back for 'em once we dump these scumbags."

Suddenly, there was no green glow on the captain's face. The lights on the control panel had flickered out.

"Get down to the engine room," the captain said, but Packer was already descending a ladder. He ran through the passenger lounge, one deck below, skirting around prisoners and corrections officers. He scurried down another ladder and another and wrenched open the hatch leading to the engine room.

He stopped. The emergency lamps were red, shedding a red glow over hundreds of barrels, the kind used to transport diesel fuel, and sitting atop the closest one, was a smallish box wrapped in silver paper and tied with a silver bow.

Packer grabbed the box and ran up three decks. The captain was still at his post, his large hands gripping the wheel. Packer gave him the gift box and reported that he saw no sign of the engine crew, just a lot of oil barrels.

The captain contacted his counterpart on the passenger ferry and outlined the situation.

The other captain's voice, issuing from the radio, was startlingly loud and clear: "Same thing over here.

Enough diesel fuel to blow us sky-high. And a present."

"Let's unwrap 'em."

Through the radio speaker, Packer and the captain heard the crackle of paper even as the captain fumbled off the silvery wrapping on the small box.

"I got a detonator," the passenger captain said. "Looks homemade."

"Yeah, me, too."

"This can't be good."

Bruce had been doing a random search of the city's transmissions when he overheard the exchange between the ferry captains. He couldn't decide if this was a lucky break or if some part of his subconscious *expected* trouble at the ferries, but it made no difference. He alerted Lucius Fox immediately, then changed into his Batman outfit.

In the main lounge of the passenger ferry, a cell phone taped to the overhead, out of anyone's reach, rang and immediately answered itself.

"Can you hear me?" the Joker asked through the ferry's speaker. "Tonight, you're all going to be part of a social experiment."

The prisoners on the first ferry were listening to the

same voice, as was Lucius Fox in the subsubbasement below the Wayne Enterprises building. Fox immediately busied himself at the console, trying to trace the call.

"Through the magic of diesel fuel and ammonium nitrate," the Joker continued, "I'm ready right now to blow you all sky-high. Anyone attempts to get off their boat, you all die. But we're going to make things a little more interesting than that. Tonight, we're going to learn a little bit about ourselves. There's no need for all of you to die. That would be a waste. So I've left you a little present. At midnight I blow you all up—both boats, boom, bye-bye. If, however, one of you presses the button, I'll let that boat live. You choose. So who's it going to be—Harvey Dent's most-wanted-scumbag collection . . . or the sweet, innocent civilians? Oh, and you might want to decide quickly, because the people on the other boat might not be so noble."

Barbara Gordon picked up the phone on the second ring. "Hello?"

"Barbara, it's Anna Ramirez. Listen carefully, there's no time. Jim needs you to pack up and get the kids in the car right away."

"But the patrol car's outside . . ."

"Barbara, those cops can't be trusted. Jim needs you away from them as soon as possible. I'll call them off for ten minutes . . . You'll have to move fast."

Ramirez was sitting at her desk in the Major Crimes Unit, hanging up her phone and wincing because Harvey Dent was pressing a gun barrel into her temple.

"She believes you?" Dent asked.

Ramirez nodded.

"She trusts you," Dent said. "Just like Rachel trusted you."

"I didn't know—"

Dent interrupted Ramirez: "—'what they were gonna do?' You're the second cop who said that to me. What, exactly, did you *think* they were going to do?"

"I'm sorry. They got me early on. My mother's medical bills—"

Dent's voice was harsh: "Don't." He flipped his coin.

Ramirez spoke rapidly: "I took a little from them, once they got you they keep you I'm sorry."

Dent caught the coin: good side.

"Live to fight another day, Officer," Dent said, and struck her with the butt of his gun.

Batman sped out into the night astride the two-wheeled pod. There was no traffic problem; the citizens had either fled or were barricaded in their dwellings.

On the freeway leading downtown, Batman spoke to Fox on his mask radio. "Anything?"

Fox did.

Batman called Gordon: "I have the Joker's location. Prewitt Building. Assemble on the building opposite."

The passengers were clustered around a National Guard commander, who had one hand on the Joker's detonator and the other on his holstered weapon. Several passengers, including a mother holding an infant and a brown-suited, gray-haired businessman, took several steps toward him.

"Stay back," the commander warned, drawing his gun.

"We don't all have to die," the mother said. "Why should my baby die? Those men had their chance . . ."

"This is not open to discussion," the commander said.

"You can bet they're discussing it on the other boat," the businessman said. "If they're even bothering to talk. Let's put it to a vote."

The crowd murmured its assent.

The businessman was wrong. On the prisoners' ferry, nobody was exactly discussing anything, though a lot of the men were muttering threats and curses as they inched forward. A corrections officer fired a shotgun blast just above their heads, then aimed the barrel of the gun directly at them. They stopped, but the muttering grew louder.

The passengers had persuaded the captain that a vote was the best way to settle their differences. Everyone tore scraps from whatever paper was available—newspaper margins, receipts, ticket stubs, old calling cards—and using either their own pens or ones borrowed from whoever was nearest, scribbled either a *yes* or a *no*. Someone provided a hat and as it was passed from person to person, each dropped their vote into it.

Ronald Coburgh stared down at the bit of paper he'd torn from a video rental card. It was blank. He looked first at the prisoner's ferry, laying maybe a hundred yards off the port bow, then at the glowing face of his watch: 11:50. Ten minutes . . .

Gordon looked at his watch—ten to midnight—then at the cops who were setting up rifle tripods on the balustrade of the building they were occupying, which was directly across from their objective.

Was Batman near? Didn't make a damn bit of difference.

The voice of a SWAT team leader called his name from his radio and said, "We found our missing school bus. Parking garage basement. Empty."

What Gordon expected and feared: a hostage situation.

He looked across the street at the Prewitt Building. The building was still under construction, and a lot of the floors were either missing or incomplete. Pipes and wiring were exposed in many areas, making the site a dangerous one. The top third of it was nothing more than steel girders forming a superstructure, gaunt against the sky; the lower section was more or less complete, at least on the outside. There were stacks of building materials littering the street, and several pieces of earthmoving equipment, and a corrugated steel trailer that served as a temporary office. Gordon knew that the job was months behind schedule and that some of the tenants had already occupied the lower, completed floors.

Several men, wearing clown masks and brandishing firearms, were standing in clear view behind one of a long row of floor-to-ceiling windows.

"It's a shooting gallery," Gordon said. "Why'd he choose a spot with such big windows."

"Maybe he likes the view," Batman said from the shadows.

"You made it," Gordon said.

Sergeant Mayer, adjusting the scope on his rifle, said: "We have clear shots on five clowns. Snipers take them out, smash the windows, a team rappels in, another team moves in by the stairwells. Two or three casualties max."

"Let's do it," Gordon said.

"It's not that simple," Batman said. "With the Joker, it never is."

"What's simple," Gordon snapped, "is that every second we don't take him, those people on the ferries get closer to blowing each other up!"

"That won't happen."

"Then he'll blow them *all* up. There's no time. We have to go in *now*."

"There's *always* a catch with him."

"That's why we can't wait, why we can't play his games—"

"I need five minutes alone." Batman retreated farther into the shadows.

"No," Gordon shouted. "There's no time. We have clear shots. Dent's in here with them. We have to save Dent. *I* have to save Dent."

Batman leapt from the building and, his cape wide, soared across the street.

Gordon turned to Mayer. "We give him two minutes. Then we breach."

Batman glided into the Prewitt Building, grabbing one of the clown-masked thugs stationed next to the window. Yanking off the clown mask, he saw that instead of one of the Joker's thugs, it was Mike Engel. Engels's hands were duct-taped together, a gun nestled between them. Looking around he saw another man in a clown mask, then realized what was going on. The Joker and his crew had put the innocent civilians in the clown masks . . . and were themselves disguised as the hostages!

A red laser dot suddenly appeared on the man's clown mask, and Batman realized the SWAT rifleman had the man in his sights. Which meant that as soon as the SWAT team fired and breached the building, dozens of innocent victims would be killed. He had to act quickly.

He tapped his connection to Lucius Fox and asked him to contact Gordon and tell him that the Joker had the hostages dressed up as clown thugs.

On the rooftop across the street, Gordon's phone rang. He glanced at the caller ID and said, "Barbara, I can't talk now."

Then he heard Harvey Dent's voice: "Hello, Jim."

"Harvey, what the hell's going on?"

"You're about to know what my suffering's really like."

Gordon peered across the street at the Prewitt Building. "Where are you. And where's my family?"

"Where *my* family died."

There was a *click*, and silence.

Sergeant Mayer looked at his watch and said, "Two minutes. Time's up. Red Team . . . go!"

———

"I couldn't reach Gordon," Lucius said into Batman's ear. "Something must be going on as he's not responding."

"Dammit," whispered Batman. "Give me sonar vision. I'll see what I can do."

"You got it."

Batman's eyes glowed white as he used his sonar to look around. Looking around and up, he saw more hostages on the floor he was on, as well as a large group gathered on the floor above, all wearing masks.

On the street, a squad of heavily armored and armed SWATs burst into the Prewitt Building.

On nearby rooftops, snipers aimed at the clowns visible through the large windows.

On the roof of the Prewitt Building, officers prepared to rappel down the wall.

A lot happened in a short time:

Batman used his grappling gun to knock three clowns to the ground, saving them from death by gunfire.

Charges set by the SWATs blasted a hole in the wall not too far from where Batman had entered the building. Batman fired his grapple gun into the lead SWAT's tear gas grenade and yanked him through the wall, smashing him into two approaching thugs dressed as doctors. He then grabbed two hostages who were in the next room and jumped down to the floor below, where he quickly dispatched several thugs dressed as doctors, nurses, and patients.

He glanced up and realized that the SWAT team was in an elevator headed to the floor above where there were more hostages dressed as thugs. But before he could do anything, the SWATs that had rappelled from the roof reached his floor and advanced on Batman. With several swift kicks and distractions he beat them back and used their rappelling rope to tie them all together.

He then aimed a device from his utility belt back up at the hostages trapped on the floor above him and fired several sticky bombs around the exposed supports near the tied-up hostages. Seconds later the bombs went off, collapsing the floor and sending the SWAT team crashing down in front of him.

Quickly recovering, the SWAT team took aim at Batman, but Batman was quicker. With a swift kick, he pushed the lead SWAT member out the window, then watched as they all fell out, one after the other, the rope attaching them all hindering them further.

Batman caught sight of the Joker and the Chechen's dogs moving swiftly above him, then fired his grapple gun up the elevator shaft in swift pursuit. He needed to end this situation as quickly as possible . . .

The captain finished counting the votes he'd collected. To push a button and kill the prisoners or trust to fate that everyone here would survive? He looked up, and said, loudly: "The tally is 196 votes against. And 340 votes for." He looked down at the detonator in his hand. "I voted for it. Same as most of you. It doesn't seem right that we should all die . . ."

"So do it!" someone yelled.

"I didn't say *I'd* do it. Don't forget—we're all still here. Which means they haven't killed us yet, either."

Everyone looked at the clock on the bulkhead: *11:59.*

The captain set the detonator down on a bench.

The gray-haired businessman picked it up and turned to address his fellow passengers. "No one wants to get his hands dirty. Fine. Those men on the other boat made their choices. They chose to murder and steal. It makes no sense for us to die, too."

No one looked at him.

He stared down at the detonator. Then he placed it on the deck and sat down on the bench.

The discussion on the other ferry was also heated. The warden still had the remote, and his hands shook when a large tattooed prisoner named Ginty approached him.

He glared down at the warden. "You don't wanna die. But you don't know how to take a life. Give it to me."

The warden looked at the timer, then back at Ginty, who still pleaded with him.

"These men will kill you and take it anyway. Give it to me. You can tell people I took it by force. Give it to me and I'll do what you should have done ten minutes ago."

The warden nodded silently and slowly handed the remote over.

Ginty walked to the nearest open porthole and threw the detonator into the bay.

Batman was certain that the hostages were safe, at least for the moment. But others, the people on the ferries—they were still in danger.

There was one place the Joker must be, where he could see all that happened and still not be caught in the chaos, and that was an office that was reached by a flight of stairs leading to a balcony. Batman was up the steps and through a door in seconds, facing the Joker.

"You came," the Joker said "I'm touched." He unleashed the Chechen's rottweilers. "Sic 'im."

The dogs leapt at Batman, hitting him hard, knocking him off his feet. He got one gauntleted arm in the jaws of the first dog and kneed the underbelly of the second, then rolled away from them.

The Joker plunged a switchblade into a crack between the sections of Batman's armor, deep into flesh and bone. He straightened up, and as Batman got to his knees, kicked, and kicked again, and Batman lurched back toward the top of one of the huge windows. The glass cracked, and a shard fell out and dropped onto the street below, but Batman caught the window frame and shoved the Joker back into the room with both his feet.

"If we don't stop fighting," the Joker said, "you're going to miss the fireworks."

"There won't *be* any fireworks."

Somewhere nearby, a tower clock began to toll midnight.

Gordon and the cops heard the clock and froze, then turned toward the bay and the two ferries, and waited. There was no explosion.

Batman faced the Joker. Both men were gasping for breath, and the Joker's makeup was smeared and streaked with sweat.

"What were you hoping to prove?" Batman asked. "That deep down we're all as ugly as you?"

The Joker held up a detonator, and with his thumb he flicked a toggle, exposing a red button. "Can't rely on anyone these days," he complained. "Have to do everything myself. I always have, and it's not always easy . . . Say, do you know how I got these scars?"

"No," Batman said, lifting his arm and shooting scallop blades out of his gauntlet. The blades struck the Joker in the chest and arm and then Batman crossed the distance between them and wrenched the detonator from the Joker's grasp. The Joker pivoted away from Batman, stumbled, fell toward the shattered window and, with a huge smile, went through it.

Batman leaned out the window, aimed his grappling gun, and fired. The rope wrapped around the Joker's leg, and Batman let him hang upside down.

"You just couldn't let me go, could you?" the Joker whined. "I guess this is what happens when an unstoppable force meets an immovable object. You are truly incorruptible, aren't you? You won't kill me out of some misplaced sense of righteousness . . . and I won't kill you because you're too much fun. We're going to do this forever."

"You'll be in a padded cell *forever*."

"Maybe we can share it. They'll have to double up, the rate this city's inhabitants are losing their minds."

"This city just showed you it's full of people ready to believe in good."

"Till their spirit breaks completely. Till they find out what I did with the best of them. Till they get a look at the *real* Harvey Dent and all the heroic things he's done. Then the criminals will be straight back onto the streets, and Gotham will understand the *true* nature of heroism.

You didn't think I'd risk losing the battle for the soul of Gotham in a fistfight, did you? You've got to have an ace in the hole. Mine's Harvey."

Batman lifted the Joker up until their faces were only inches apart. "What did you do?"

"I took Gotham's white knight and I brought him down to my level. It wasn't hard. Madness is like gravity—all it takes is a little push."

The Joker laughed, and continued laughing as Batman used plastic ties to secure him to a radiator. The SWAT team would find him in a minute or two.

Batman grabbed the upper windowsill ledge and swung himself out and up. He somersaulted onto the roof and used his radio to tell Lucius Fox to locate Harvey Dent.

Gordon didn't know how it had all happened, or even exactly *what* had happened, just that, somehow, for some reason, about ten of his best men had been taken down, though none was hurt seriously, and that neither ferry had blown up, and that the Joker was just taken into custody. Maybe he would *never* know, and he didn't care, not right now. He had something else to worry about, something that had formed a cold lump in his belly, and so, without waiting for anyone's report, he ran to his car. He paused only long enough to tell Sergeant Mayer where he was going, and to ask Mayer to send some units when things had calmed down at the Prewitt Building. Then he put on his siren and sped toward Second Avenue. Maybe he should wait for backup, maybe he should bring someone, maybe he should try to contact Batman . . . Maybe maybe maybe.

Dent had said that Gordon's wife and son were "where my family died." Dent's family? What did he know about Dent's family? A second cousin in Dubuque, an aunt in Fairbanks—both alive, as far as Gordon knew, and Dent wasn't close to either one, anyway. That meant . . . what? Where Rachel Dawes had died. It was all Gordon could think of. He turned the car around and headed for the warehouse. Minutes later, he entered the blackened wreck of a building, gun in one hand, flashlight in the other.

He called Dent's name and waited. Nothing.

Gordon moved farther into the building, his shoes crunching on debris, his flashlight playing over gaunt, charred beams. He rounded a corner and there they were, Barbara and his son and daughter, huddled together near a jagged black hole where the floor had collapsed. Barbara was shaking her head *no*, but he didn't understand her until he heard footsteps behind him. He started to turn, and something hit him behind his left ear. He went down, but not quite out, and felt rough hands take his gun and roll him onto his back. He looked up. Moonlight was streaming through a gap in the ceiling, illuminating Harvey Dent, who was holding a revolver, his face canted a bit so that only the right side was revealed. It was a pleasant, handsome face, and Dent spoke in his lawyer's voice—strong, reasonable.

"This is where they brought her, Gordon. After your people handed her over. This is where they bound her. This is where she suffered. This is where she died."

"I know. I was here, trying to save her."

Dent moved his head a few inches, and now the charred and twisted left side was showing. He said, "But you didn't, did you?"

"I couldn't."

"Yes, you could. If you'd listened to me, if you'd stood up against corruption instead of doing your deal with the devil—"

"I was trying to fight the mob."

"You wouldn't dare try to justify yourself if you knew what I lost. Have you ever had to talk to the person you love most, wondering if you're about to listen to them die? You ever had to lie to that person? Tell them it's going to be all right, when you know it's not? Well, you're about to find out what that feels like. *Then* you'll be able to look me in the eyes and tell me you're sorry!"

Dent stepped to Barbara, nudged her closer to the hole in the floor, and put his gun to her temple.

"Harvey, put the gun down. You're not going to hurt my family."

"No, just the person you need most. So is it your wife?" Dent aimed his weapon at the little girl, then at the boy.

"Godammit, stop pointing the gun at my family," Gordon shouted.

"We have a winner," Dent said. He pulled the boy away from his mother.

"No!" Barbara screamed. "Jim, stop him! Don't let him!"

"I'm sorry, Harvey," Gordon said. "For everything. But please, please don't hurt him."

Batman was experiencing flashes of dizziness, and he felt sticky warmth trickling down his skin from where the Joker had stabbed him. *This* wound was not superficial. He needed help. He wondered how much blood he'd lost, how long he could continue before exhaustion and trauma would buckle his knees, would sweep a red fog over his vision. Not long, but maybe long enough.

He could hear Gordon's voice somewhere ahead, in the charred ruins. They were near, the ones he had to rescue, all of them, the Gordons and Harvey Dent, and maybe in saving them, he could save himself.

Dent stopped, cocked his head, and listened. There was the wail of police sirens, drawing closer.

Dent looked down at Gordon. "You brought your *cops*?"

"All they know is there's a situation. They don't know who, or what. They're just creating a perimeter."

"You think I want to *escape*? There's no escape from *this*." He thrust a finger into his left cheek.

Gordon spoke earnestly, calmly. "There's no need to escape because nobody's done anything wrong. And nobody has to."

Dent chuckled. "I've done plenty wrong, Gordon. Just not quite enough. *Yet*."

"Let him go. You're right. It's *my* fault Rachel died. Punish *me*."

"I'm about to," Dent said.

The boy whimpered as Dent pressed the gun into his neck.

Batman stepped from the darkness into the moonlight, and said, "You don't want to hurt the boy, Dent."

"It's not about what *I* want," Dent said. "It's about what's *fair*. You thought we could be decent men in an indecent world. You thought we could lead by example. You thought the rules could be bent but not break . . . You were *wrong*. The world is cruel." Dent removed his coin from a pocket. "And the only morality in a cruel world is chance. Unbiased. Unprejudiced. *Fair*."

"Nothing fair ever came out of the barrel of a gun, Dent," said Batman.

"His boy's got the same chance she had. Fifty-fifty."

"What happened to Rachel wasn't chance. We decided to act. We three. We knew the risks and we acted as one. We are all responsible for the consequences."

Dent looked pleadingly at Batman. "Then why was it only *me* who lost everything?"

"It wasn't."

"The Joker chose *me*!"

"Because you were the *best* of us. He wanted to prove that even someone as good as you could fall."

Dent's voice sounded bitter. "And he was *right*."

Batman shook his head. "You're fooling yourself if you think you're letting chance decide. *You're* the one pointing the gun, Harvey. So point it at the people who were responsible. We all acted as one. Gordon. Me. And you."

"Fair enough," Dent said, stepping away from the boy. "You first."

He aimed his gun at Batman and flipped the coin: bad side. He fired, and Batman dropped, clutching his midsection.

"My turn." Dent put the gun against his temple and flipped the coin: good side.

He pointed the gun at Gordon's son, and said, "Your turn, Gordon. Tell your son it's going to be all right, Gordon. *Lie*. Like I lied."

"It's going to be all right, son," Gordon said.

Gordon and Barbara and Dent all watched the coin spinning in the air, so they didn't see Batman roll into a kneel and spring at Dent and the boy. The three of them, locked together in Batman's arms, toppled over the edge of the hole and into the darkness below.

The coin landed.

Gordon grabbed his flashlight and shined it into the

hole. At the bottom, Dent was sprawled, neck twisted, the mutilated side of his face exposed, his left eye open and staring sightlessly. He was obviously dead.

But where were the others?

"Help," he heard Batman say.

Gordon swept his light and saw Batman hanging from a charred joist with his left hand, while his right clutched the boy. Gordon set his flashlight on the floor and reached down to take his son from Batman.

His flashlight was shining on Dent's coin: good side.

The joist Batman hung from snapped, loud as a gunshot, and Batman fell, smashing through wood and plumbing, landing hard next to Dent.

Gordon gave the boy to Barbara and hesitated.

"You've got to help him," Barbara said.

Gordon ran down the stairs, occasionally jumping past heaps of debris and through the door into the basement—the place where Rachel Dawes had died.

Batman was moving. Gordon helped him to his feet, and said, "Thank you."

"You don't have to—"

"Yes, I do."

Both men gazed down at Dent's body, pale and still in the moonlight.

"The Joker won," Gordon said. "Harvey's prosecution, everything he fought for, everything Rachel died for . . . Undone. Whatever chance Gotham had of fixing itself . . . whatever chance you gave us of fixing our city, dies with Harvey's reputation. We bet it all on him. The Joker took the best of us and tore him down. People will lose all hope."

"No, they won't. They can never know what he did."

Gordon was incredulous. "But we can't sweep that under the—"

"No," Batman said, his voice overriding Gordon's. "The Joker *cannot* win." He crouched by Dent's body and gently turned Dent's head until the unmarred side was visible. "Gotham needs its true hero."

"I don't understand—" Gordon stopped, and stared at Batman. "You?" he asked finally. "You can't—"

"Yes, I can."

Batman rose and faced Gordon. "You either die a hero or live long enough to see yourself become a villain. I can do those things because I'm not a hero, like Dent. *I* killed those people. That's what I can be."

"No," Gordon said angrily. "You can't. You're not!"

"I'm whatever Gotham needs me to be."

"They'll hunt you."

"*You'll* hunt me. You'll condemn me, set the dogs on me because it's what needs to happen. Because sometimes the truth isn't good enough. Sometimes, people deserve more."

Gordon turned his back on Batman and stood unmoving until he was sure he was alone with Harvey

Dent's body. Then he slowly trudged up the three flights of steps and rejoined his family.

"Why did Batman run away?" Gordon's son asked him.

"Because we have to chase him."

"Why?"

EPILOGUE

Blood formed a wet film beneath his clothing, and the red fog he'd feared was exploding behind his eyes. But he might be able to reach somewhere he could rest, allow himself a few moments peace before his long nightmare began. He had failed to save Harvey Dent, had failed to save Rachel. But perhaps he could still put himself on the side of the angels by allowing the world to believe him to be the ugliest of devils.

Why, the child had asked. *Why did Batman run away?*

And as Batman crossed the rooftops of the sleeping city, not sure where he was going, knowing only that his wounds were deep and would never heal, James Gordon tried to answer his son's question:

He's the hero Gotham deserves, but not the one it needs right now. So we'll hunt him because he can take it. Because he's not our hero, he's a silent guardian, a watchful protector . . . a dark knight.